Night Gardening

This Large Print Book carries the
Seal of Approval of N.A.V.H.

Night Gardening

$E. L. S$wann

G.K. Hall & Co. • Thorndike, Maine

Excerpts from *The Education of a Gardener* by Russell Page copyright © 1962, 1983 by Russell Page. Reprinted by permission of Random House, Inc.

Excerpts from *Contemplative Gardens* by Julie Moir Messervy copyright © 1990 by Julie Moir Messervy. Reprinted by permission of the author.

Excerpt from *The Inward Garden* by Julie Moir Messervy reprinted by permission of Little, Brown and Company.

Excerpt from *The Secret Life of a Garden* by Stephen Dalton copyright © 1992 by Calman & King, Ltd. Reprinted by permission of the Overlook Press.

Excerpt from *Japanese Stone Gardens: How to Make Them and Enjoy Them* copyright Kazuhiko Fukudo. Reprinted by permission of Charles E. Tuttle, Inc.

Published in 2000 by arrangement with Hyperion, an imprint of Buena Vista Books, Inc.

G.K. Hall Large Print Core Series.

The text of this Large Print edition is unabridged.
Other aspects of the book may vary from the original edition.

Set in 16 pt. Plantin by Elena Picard.

Printed in the United States on permanent paper.

Library of Congress Cataloging-in-Publication Data

Swann, E. L.
    Night gardening / E.L. Swann.
      p. cm.
    ISBN 0-7838-9036-2 (lg. print : hc : alk. paper)
    1. Cerebrovascular disease — Patients — Fiction. 2. Landscape
architects — Fiction. 3. Middle aged persons — Fiction.
4. Cambridge (Mass.) — Fiction. 5. Widows — Fiction.
6. Large type books.
PS3561.N485 N54 2000
   813'.54—dc21
                                    00-029570

To C. G. K.

If I cannot accept
the real as real
then how do I accept
a dream as a dream?

PRIEST SAIGYO,
AN ITINERANT TWELFTH-
CENTURY POET MONK

CHAPTER 1

Tristan Mallory

If you wish to make anything grow you must understand it, and you must understand it in a very real sense.

RUSSELL PAGE,
The Education of a Gardener

Tristan Mallory looked in the rearview mirror of his truck as he switched lanes. Good. Peter, with Roger, just two cars behind, was negotiating to get into the right lane. Hopefully he would not miss the exit for 93 as he did last time. The notion of a nineteen-year-old kid endlessly circling Boston on Route 128 with a hundred thousand dollars' worth of grading equipment in a truck was an unsettling one. Tristan himself hauled a few tons of stone, a remarkable stone that was the offspring of the geological version of a shotgun marriage, first forged in some Paleozoic cauldron when an ocean plate took a dive into a trench and came up with scraps from which the future Appalachian and Caledonian mountains would be built. When Scotland, along with the rest of Europe, decided to break off from North

America and sail majestically eastward at the stately pace of a few inches per millennium, this lovely deep gray stone with slate blue markings was left on both edges of the newly formed continents.

Last night, Tristan had talked with Luigi, who had promised to have his men there to help with the unloading. Luigi would then cut the stones so that Tristan could lay them in a half-split half-saw pattern, which he felt gave a lovely texture to paths in lawns that tended toward the overly manicured, as was the case with this garden.

These were nice people, the Steins. Recently moved from New York, they had seen Tristan's work in Litchfield, Connecticut, and some gardens in the Hamptons on Long Island. But Tristan always worried about women who wanted to do white gardens, renditions of Vita Sackville-West's white garden at Sissinghurst. That was what Judith Stein wanted. It wasn't that he objected to relying on someone else's original inspiration. The women were always careful to say that they did not want an exact copy and assured him that it was to have his indelible stamp. He always wondered what they thought his indelible stamp was.

No, it was not the ghosts of Sackville-West and Sissinghurst gardens that disturbed him. It was the women's own ghosts that he worried about. What was haunting these suddenly rich women who often had come from very simple backgrounds? Was he being overly romantic, or

10

hadn't these women often grown up in places where folks had patios with whiskey tubs spilling with petunias and creeping phlox, or nice little kitchen gardens stuffed with cherry tomato plants, herbs, and lettuces; or, maybe, even farms with fields of corn, soy beans, and alfalfa, and then, too, half-acre vegetable plots crawling with melons and sprouting trellises of pole beans. All of them good honest gardens. Tristan didn't get it. Didn't they want to hang on to any of those first connections with flowers, things blooming, the earth? Where the hell did they come up with Sissinghurst? Tristan wondered if these women had any stories of their own to tell in their gardens, any real narratives. It was almost as if once these women had arrived at the lifestyles they had so rigorously sought, married the men who could buy them everything, they gave up their own stories. The gardens seem to come to the women as full-blown ideas in their heads, independent of their own personal histories or even the particular landscape or countryside where they would grow. It became a dangerous business in which gardens were not shaped by topography and soil but were inflicted upon a landscape.

The Sullivan Square exit was coming up. Peter was right behind him now. Miss this one and you're headed for the Cape. The down ramp was clear at this early hour of the morning and they were soon cutting across Somerville to Cambridge. Tristan always marveled at how quickly

11

the entire feeling changed once one crossed the Somerville-Cambridge line. Seedy mom-and-pop shops vanished. Furniture stores with horrendously ugly bedroom sets crammed into windows gave way to discreet emporiums for buying bread or exotic coffee beans. The concrete sidewalks turned into brick ones. Students, elderly professors with berets, and stout well-shod older ladies with dogs on leashes could be spotted on every corner. Tristan made it a point, even early in the morning, to avoid Harvard Square. So he turned away from the square and went instead around the Cambridge Common. Then he turned down Mason Street which took him in one short block on to hallowed Brattle Street, Tory Row as it had once been called in its colonial days. The largest houses with the largest trees were on Brattle. No property here could be touched for under a million these days. It was the address to have in Cambridge.

Equally expensive and prestigious were homes on the two or three cul-de-sacs directly off Brattle. The Steins had gotten their hands on one of these, a real showcase. Designed by H. H. Richardson in the late 1800s, the house was a sprawling shingled behemoth with twenty-five rooms. There was a deep backyard with easy access for bulldozers, backhoes, and any of the heavy scraping equipment that Tristan wanted to use. A landscaper's dream in terms of access. Too bad that Judith Stein didn't want to do more with really big rocks — a Japanese garden. He could have brought in some five-ton granite beauties and created something worthy of a Japanese silk scroll.

There were only two other houses on the cul-de-sac, an imposing Federal-style clapboard, dating earlier than the Richardson, and then a stucco, rather elegant if slightly past its prime even though thirty years younger than the other two. The walls of the stucco were the color of cognac and they crawled with ivy that threaded through the dark green shutters, threatening to pull them off their hinges. The tarnished brass knocker on the front door appeared as if it might groan from disuse rather than actually knock. The house itself seemed to crouch in the shadows of the Richardson. Still it had character, a somewhat mysterious quality to it that always caused Tristan to pause a moment as he pulled up to the Steins.

He would hate to think of a white garden in a place like the stucco house. There were of course very few places in a city, even a small city like Cambridge, that would lend themselves to wildness, but this one, the stucco, possibly could. Even in the most formal of gardens there was, in Tristan's mind, always room for something a little unkempt, a little wild — a woodland corner, perhaps, sequestered somewhere within the shadows.

Luigi was waiting for him, as was a truck with a half ton of crushed gravel. Tristan reached over the back of his seat, fished out the cardboard tube with the site plans, and got out of the truck. He was tall, his silvery hair close cropped. His face already tan from the spring work was scored by white squint lines that flared from his eyes to his temples. He didn't wear his sunglasses as he had when he was younger because he needed his reading glasses to look at the plans. Sometimes he resorted to wearing his reading glasses under his sunglasses but that could be awkward.

"Buon giorno, Luigi."

"How ya doin', Mr. Mallory. Here, I want you to meet my nephew Al and my other nephew Gian Franco, and here's my wife's younger brother — you know Tony, he was on that job with us in Concord."

"Oh sure, Tony. How ya doin'?" Tristan shook hands. Luigi had an endless supply of nephews and brothers and brothers-in-law and cousins. They came in various sizes and shapes and all were adept with stone — wrestling, lifting, cutting, and shaping it. "So where you got your shop set up?"

"Out back," Luigi said, pointing, "where the lower terrace will be. Good water source. Don't even have to use the longest extensions. Terrific access. Place like this — I would have never believed it — not in Cambridge."

"Well, for what they paid for this place they should have good access," Tristan replied.

"What'd ya say the guy does, Mr. Mallory?"

"Investment banking."

"Ah, that explains it. How come he's not living in Wellesley? That's where the bankers all live — Wellesley and Dover."

"Don't ask me." Tristan shrugged.

The men walked around to the backyard. It was just 7:30 in the morning and Tristan was pleased to see that the tracked bulldozer he had rented from Perrelli Construction was already there. It crouched like a sleeping beast in the middle of the leveled space awaiting its first command. The grade stakes were all still in place but Tristan would check them again. On a huge mound of stripped-off topsoil a woman in her early forties stood in a raincoat. The hem of her nightgown showed. She held a mug of coffee in her hand as she surveyed her domain, now scraped bare. The featureless expanse was interrupted only by the tracked bulldozer and then the scoring of trenches for utilities — pipes and electrical cables.

"Hello, Mrs. Stein."

"Judith please, Tristan, call me Judith."

"Okay, Judith. Well, today it begins." And as if on cue a tinkety staccato cough of the Alden grader starting up fractured the stillness of the morning. From the rear access lane behind the property the yellow claws appeared. Then underneath the claws there was a set of adjustable blades.

"What's that?" Judith Stein asked.

"Kind of cute, isn't it? Like a baby dinosaur.

15

It's our favorite high-wheeled grader. Your boys up yet?"

"Oh yeah."

"Well, get them out here. This is their day. You should let them skip school. It's a Tonka toy dream come true today."

Judith Stein smiled. Tristan was looking out at the machinery that Peter and Roger were driving into the yard. Tanned already, with deep vertical lines scoring his cheeks and that silvery gray hair, Tristan Mallory wasn't hard to look at. She wondered how old he was. At least sixty. "Do you have children?" she asked.

"I've got grandchildren," he replied.

"They must love having a grandfather like you."

"Don't get to see them enough. They live out in California. I go holidays, but it's not the same." Tristan wasn't sure what he meant by "the same." He figured that people do not precisely imagine their lives as grandparents, but having raised his daughters by himself since they were fairly young he had, he supposed, thought of the grandchildren just being nearby, constantly around. He had made how many thousands of foldover jelly sandwiches for the girls? And now it occurred to him that he had never made any for little Tristan, or Timmy, or Mary. There was a small twinge someplace deep inside, and then suddenly he felt ridiculous. He turned abruptly to Judith Stein. "Have you talked to the people next door about the wall yet?"

16

"Bill has a date tonight to talk with her children. She hasn't been well. Actually it's the son he's going to talk to. The woman, Mrs. Welles, is a widow. We haven't met her since we moved in."

"The wall hasn't been well for a long time. We've reinforced it as best we can from this side," Tristan said. "I mean it's a pretty wall, the faded brick, the coping on top. You don't want to take it down entirely. Seems like they should share the costs of doing a really nice job on it."

It seemed like an unimportant issue to Judith Stein whether they shared in the costs or not. "If they don't want to it's no problem. We'll take care of the whole thing."

He knew they would. These were the kind of people who just did not consider that money should ever be an obstacle to anything.

"Well, got to get to work." He sidestepped nimbly down the steep slope of topsoil and walked in long graceful strides across the bare ground toward the two young men who stood by the scraper and the Bobcat. Judith Stein watched as he unfurled a set of plans and began pointing at grading sticks that marked the property. She closed her eyes a moment and willed a vision of the central arbor at Sissinghurst laden with alabaster *Rosa mulliganii.*

CHAPTER 2

Maggie Welles

"Green Fingers" are a fact, and a mystery only to the unpracticed. But green fingers are the extensions of a verdant heart.

RUSSELL PAGE,
The Education of a Gardener

Maggie Welles sat in her wheelchair in the sun room. She was lost in one of the peculiar reveries that had become commonplace since her stroke. She was thinking about noses — Welles noses, to be precise. When she had first met her late husband Adams Welles, a senior at Harvard at the time, he had a thin, delicately arched nose, the same as his brother who was just a year older and a younger sister and assorted cousins. Their noses were so fine, so aristocratic, as if designed to sniff and never to snort, to inhale only the most delicate of fragrances. But all the Welleses, including most certainly her husband, drank. Yet, even after several martinis at lunch, they could still hit a golf ball straight down the fairway, in a flash add up a check, and figure their customary 12 percent tip, which drove

Maggie nuts. They could drive cars, recall parts of ridiculous old songs and poems, never slurring a word and never exhibiting any shred of inappropriate behavior. They were perfect drunks, unlike, say, the Kennedys. It never showed — except in their noses.

The Welles noses simply grew redder and more disfigured through the years. One could trace it — the bright red tint set in sometime in their mid-twenties, just a couple of years after she and Adams had married. By their early thirties the first little burst of veins appeared, blossoming like miniature fireworks and usually favoring the left side of the nose. Then the lumps, small as blisters in the beginning, progressing through their forties until by their mid-fifties, no trace of the original elegantly arched nose was left. Instead there was this slightly smashed, red lumpy thing that had taken on a character of its own in the middle of the face. One could almost say that among Welles men their noses often had more personality than any other part of them. The Welles women were let off slightly easier. Their noses turned red but were not quite so disfigured, and of course makeup helped.

Maggie had watched those noses over thirty years of their marriage and found a deep irony in it that she only now allowed herself to fully enjoy. She, after all, was the Irish one. Adams Welles had married down when he fell for Maggie Flaherty, straight out of Boston's most Irish neighborhood, Charlestown. Charlestown — less than two miles but a world away from Beacon Hill, Cambridge, and the other haunts of Brahmin Boston. Her mother had worked as the housekeeper at the Porcellian Club, the most August of Harvard's social clubs known as finals. On one occasion Maggie had been asked by her mother to come and help serve at a spring dinner. She had to wear a black uniform and a starched white apron. She refused to wear the little white headpiece. She was beautiful. Dark red hair, green eyes, with a slight upward tilt, like so many of her relatives from County Clare. She was a sophomore at Regis College, a Catholic women's school in the Boston area. She had won a St. Anthony's scholarship to the school. That plus money from her parish, not to mention Monsignor John frequently slipping her a twenty-dollar bill, covered her tuition and books. She still lived at home. It wasn't just money. She was her parents' only child and they were loath for her to move into a dormitory.

That evening at Porcellian, four different fellows had asked her for dates. But Adams was the one she accepted. First of all, he wasn't drunk even though she had refilled his glass several times and then after the dinner she had kept pouring brandies for him. He was also the kindest. She could tell that right off. Not very smart, however. She learned that later. It had come as a surprise. She naturally thought that all Harvard men were smart. She soon found out

23

that such was not always the case, especially when the men came from old and very rich Harvard families with distinguished records of giving to the school.

The Welles family, after generations of marrying cousins and relying on the brains of its founding members, had little to recommend itself other than its distinguished lineage and consistent generosity to Harvard over the years. But, as Maggie discovered, deals had been systematically brokered throughout several decades to admit decidedly less-than-sterling Welles intellects into Harvard. Their own son Adams Welles, the fifth, had barely made it through and was told to not even bother applying to the business school. Undoubtedly drinking had taken its toll on the family, even though they rarely betrayed any sign of it in a social context. They just did not have the sharpness, the ingenuity of the old founding fathers who had the foresight to buy prime real estate before it was prime, to figure out their niche in the wool market or, for that matter, the opium trade in China. There had been a time when the Welleses had been reliant on drugs in a different manner. They had not simply taken drugs but sold them. There were no red noses back then. Much of the Welleses' original fortune had indeed been made in opium, like so many other prominent New England families in the early to mid-nineteenth century. In the last seventy-five years poor financial planning coupled with unwise real estate

24

ventures and other schemes had definitely de-
pleted the coffers of some of the Welleses.

Maggie had thought about these Welles noses
a lot lately. She was sure that had she been of a
statistical or mathematical bent, she could have
plotted the tumescence of the noses in correla-
tion to the detumescence of the penises of Welles
men. Convergent pathologies, is that what they
would have called it? The last time Maggie had
sexual intercourse with her fully tumescent
spouse was when she was forty-six years old.
There had been fumbling attempts sporadically
over the next few years but none in the last two
years of her husband's life. He died at fifty-nine,
flaccid in every sense of the word. Maggie was
now sixty-one.

"You want to go outside, Mrs. Welles? It's a
nice sunny day. I'll wheel you out. Miss Roberts
isn't to come for another half hour. She could
work with you out there."

Maggie looked up at Suzy. Suzy, the day girl,
was a physical paradox. Slight, fragile with wispy
blonde hair, she packed amazing muscle into an
unpreposessing body. She was the one who got
her up in the morning, washed her, got her
dressed. Maggie opened her mouth to speak but
once more the glass wall came down. No, she
would not use the notebook to write. That alone
would tire her out. But how to frame up all these
thoughts? How could there be so much information when just a simple yes or no was required?
What she wanted to say was that it would be too

noisy out there when Miss Roberts, the speech therapist, arrived. And there might be a wind so she wouldn't be able to do the candle exercise where she puffed on the flame until it blew out.

Those were the two practical reasons not to go outside. The other reason she resisted was that it was just too painful for her to watch what promised to be an extraordinary garden being created next door while her own garden languished like some invalid, turning first brown, then gray. Now it was beyond the invalid stage. It was a carcass, definitely dead but not quite fossilized. There had been a bad drought the summer before her stroke. That had not helped things, but the real problem was the absolutely ridiculous financial stipulations Adams had left in his will which only allocated fifteen hundred dollars a year for the garden's maintenance. You could do little more than cut the grass and fertilize for that. No, she must discipline herself not to think about that. It was too maddening.

She must instead concentrate on forming her thoughts into words. She must get through this glass wall. Now what did Miss Roberts say? "Frame the thought." A single thought. And since her reading and writing skills remained intact she could try and picture the spelling of the word. *Nnn.* Her tongue was thick in her mouth. It was as if she were stirring the heaviest, lumpiest batter in the world. She pressed her tongue to the roof of her mouth then dropped it and opened her mouth a bit. "Feel the air come in,"

Miss Roberts had said. "Noise." Maggie spoke the single word. It was rather like magic once the thought had been framed — the single word was out and the rest followed with relative ease. The words still sounded thick with a bass undertone and they came slowly, but she could speak.

"Noise?" replied Suzy.

"Yes, too m-much noise, dear. All the w-work next door, you know-w."

"Oh, they've finished with the big equipment. Tractor and all that. They're just spreading stuff around with rakes now and laying stone paths. Dug a little pond."

"I . . . I . . . used to have a p-pond here. The l-lining — cement — it cr-cracked." She giggled ferociously and her tongue slipped out of her mouth. She quickly swallowed just like Miss Roberts had told her. Once before when she had laughed she had bitten her tongue so hard it bled. The reason she giggled was that she had thought of a joke. She had wanted to say "cracked like my head." Maggie had a hundred little dark jokes about her brain and what had happened.

On a night in August — eight months before — something queer had occurred inside Maggie's brain. A cerebral drama was how she thought of it, but the doctors had uniquely ugly sounding words for what had happened: "right-hemisphere hemorrhagic infarct": fart in the brain. That was Maggie's first joke about her stroke. Her children didn't get it. In fact, they did not take it as a joke at all. They thought it was an indication that something much worse had happened than just a cataract of blood pouring through her brain. "Most people who have had strokes slur words," her daughter Ceil had said. "Mother does that and talks dirty, too." The doctor had told them there could be personality changes due to the stroke. The children blinked. The two Welles children, having personalities that ranged somewhere between bland and austere, hardly knew how to assess this bit of information. Their mother had always been a little different from the rest of them, and now she would apparently be even more so. They just hoped it wouldn't be too embarrassing.

CHAPTER 3

Sounds Through the Wall

Any starting point will do — a seedling in a three-inch flower pot to grow into a magic bean stalk up which we can climb to open a gate into another aspect of this world.

RUSSELL PAGE,
The Education of a Gardener

Whhhyyyyy . . . arrrghhh. It was a painful noise that seeped through the wall. Tristan on his knees looked up from the soil sample he had just begun to take from the newly graded ground. The sound came again. He wasn't sure whether it was animal or human. He was alone in the garden now. The others, Peter and Roger and Luigi's crew, had gone to pick up sandwiches in Harvard Square. Tristan had decided not to go. Yesterday he had gone to pick up a sandwich and was accosted by a mime. In general Tristan had a low tolerance for street entertainers, but he absolutely hated mimes. His stomach curdled as these genderless beings pranced up to him, getting into his face with their chalky white ones. He hated their cloying little gestures, the choreography of their white-gloved hands. He always had this urge to scream "Shut up!" at them, which of course was exactly what they were already doing. So instead, yesterday, he had just muttered "Beat it!" He imagined this could have been grounds for capital punishment in Harvard Square.

From the other side of the garden wall came a strange noise. Not a mime. There was a definite sound, a voice of something had barked. Was it a cry or a word trying to be formed? It seemed disembodied. It was almost a weathering sound, like wind around the eaves of a house. But it was a windless April day. Tristan got up and walked toward the wall. The wall itself was at least eight feet high and the crack began a foot or more from the top and then widened. He peered through. He caught his breath. A mist seemed to hang over the backyard — everything was either gray or a hazy brown. Bushes and shrubs were still a wintry dun. The climbing roses, left to go wild, crawled over everything. Peter had clipped some of these vines that had cast themselves over the wall to the Steins' side. Now he saw that all of them were leafless and without the promise of a bud.

The trees in the garden were shrouded in sinewy tangles of ivy, myrtle, even wild grape. And it was evident that *Acre sedum,* wall pepper, with its trailing stems that can root instantaneously anywhere, was choking everything else out. A stand of peonies was making a valiant effort, but this June would be their last season to bloom if the wall pepper kept coming.

"It's like Sherman's march," Tristan whispered to himself. And indeed he felt as if he were looking at a ruin, a beautiful ruin of ineffable mystery. A haunted garden with a strange indefinable sweetness at its very center. Old trees, a copper beech, Norway and Japanese maples, an ancient horse chestnut, all impervious to the insults of neglect, reached out across what had been the center space of the garden to touch one another — like fingers on the hands of long-lost friends. And Tristan bet that the center space had never been a pristine lawn, mown and fed, laced with broad leaf killer, and cut to perfection. No. It probably had winding pea gravel paths arched over by the elegant branches of the old trees. There would have been islands of ornamental grass perhaps. The mantle of dense and quite dead-looking vegetation was so heavy that one could hardly see the center. A variety of plants had run amok in snarling tangles — barberry, honeysuckle brambles galore, weeds, and woodbine.

It was a large garden and toward the rear in one corner, huge gray barked trees stood sacred and remote like Druids from a misty past. Tristan could imagine trillium and bluebells at their feet and carpets of mosses. And yes, perhaps a moss-covered stone bench. How far gone was it, he wondered. Then he heard the strange sound again and his eyes followed it.

On a terrace, filigreed in shade cast by a

copper beech, a woman sat slumped in a wheel-chair. She wore sunglasses and was wrapped in a shawl. Another woman, dressed in some kind of uniform, came bustling out. She carried a tray with a candle on it.

Tristan, relieved to see that someone was in attendance and the woman in the wheelchair was not in any kind of state of emergency, could not help but wonder about the tray with the candle. Was some ritual about to take place? He shrank back a bit from the crack in the wall.

Maggie was irritated as she saw Miss Roberts coming from the house. Why was she so prompt? And why was she wearing that uniform? She would ask her. She got ready to frame the words *why are. Whyyyy arrrghh.* They came out mangled. She sighed and tried again. Usually Miss Roberts ran a bit late, giving her a little more peeking time through the crack in the wall. She had barely had time to get her first glimpse through the crack before Miss Roberts arrived and she had tried to frame that question. But Suzy had been right. The noise of the heavy machinery had abated, except for the occasional groans of a backhoe, and what it had wrought was somewhat of a miracle in less than seven days. This landscape team had God beat as far as Maggie was concerned. The hideous old red-wood deck with the grotesque ramada had been demolished. The lawn flanked on two sides with the ugliest perennial borders imaginable had been stripped out. The rock garden, which had never been great, had been bulldozed. In its place was a newly shaped world. From her vantage point, Maggie could see fragments of it. There was a sunken terrace, led to by a long walk of beautiful flagstones which was in the process of being laid out. Off this long walk, Maggie could see strings outlining the perimeter of little "garden rooms." At the end of the sunken garden she could glimpse what appeared to be a cliff in the making, constructed out of some wonderful granite boulders. She had seen the man in the blue shirt with the silver hair out there directing their placement a few days before. She liked watching him do this. He looked like a conductor leading an orchestra through an adagio section of a symphony. His long lithe figure swayed a bit and his arms were delicate in their movements as he guided the Bobcat with its half ton load. She hoped he would put in some more rocks today. She would get Suzy to move her chair into a better position for viewing.

"Hello, Mrs. Welles."

"Whyyy are you here so earl-l-y and whyyy are you wearing that uniform?"

"Good for you, Mrs. Welles."

"Answer-r the question!" Maggie snapped.

Miss Roberts smiled. "I have to go over to Mass General Hospital right after this, that's why. I am required to wear the uniform there when I work with patients." Maggie nodded.

"Let's light the candle while the wind is

down," Miss Roberts said.

"Yes." Maggie said the word precisely now, with the correct sibilance that would perhaps make the flame of the candle waver. Miss Roberts smiled again. The dear woman was trying harder these days. She had made remarkable strides in just the past week. At first Miss Roberts had balked at working with her in the garden. Felt there might be too many distractions and it had proved quite difficult when the work crew were using some of their machinery. She struck the match. "Shall we begin?"

Maggie leaned forward to the flame.

"Not too close, you'll burn yourself."

Issssn't it funny
How a bear likes honey . . .

"Good! Good, Mrs. Welles! Now really make that flame go out with the zzz's."

Maggie continued.

Buzz buzz buzz
I wonder why he does?

Tristan Mallory was mesmerized as he watched the scene through the crack in the wall. Some of the woody vines of the roses had crawled through the crack, so he took out his small nippers and cut them. Then he crouched down toward the bottom where some more had crept through and clipped those, too. The view was improved. He stayed in this position and watched. He wished the woman would take off her sunglasses. He'd like to see her face. The woman's left forearm hung loosely off the arm-rest of the chair, and her hair, piled up and un-kempt, looked somewhat like an abandoned bird's nest. Despite all this there was an elegance about her even as she slumped in her chair.

A large portion of the crack in the wall was now filled with blue. Was the man in the blue shirt fixing the wall? Maggie hoped not. For years she had railed about its condition, but now she rather enjoyed the view it gave her. Just as she was being taught to frame her thoughts for ex-pression into words, the crack was letting her frame small pieces of a new world beyond the garden. She actually did not want the whole view. Panoramas no longer interested Maggie. It was the small pieces, the narrow slices of reality that she found the most engaging. The rest was apt to disappoint. There had been some talk, however, about repairing the wall. Her daughter and son, Ceil and Adams Jr., had apparently met with the Steins the previous evening to discuss it. What was there to discuss? Masonry costs money. They'd blow the entire year's garden budget on the wall. She doubted that her chil-dren would contribute, and now that was fine with her. She saw the blue move up in the crack and then a pant leg.

"Now did you bring something to read to me,

Mrs. Welles? You said that Winnie the Pooh was becoming boring. You wanted something more exciting."

"Yes-ss, in my bag on the b-b-ack of the wheel-chair."

"You know, Mrs. Welles, Elsie Lavin, your physical therapist, is jealous of me?"

"Whhyyyy zzzz that?"

"Look at you — just popping out those three hard words — your tongue light as a butterfly over all those hard sounds. That's why she is jealous. She thinks you could be doing much more in the walking department."

"Walking talking . . . one thhhhing at a time."

"Don't you want to walk more? You could use the walker and then a cane."

"Where w-would I walk to?"

"Where would you like to walk?"

"In my g-garden but the paths are a m-mess. I would f-fall."

Tristan could hear every thick word of the woman's speech. It sounded as if she had something gooey in her mouth. Her tongue like a heavy blade trying to stir it, but he could hear it and he had been right: there had been paths in the garden.

"So this is what you brought to read, a wild-flower guide. How interesting." She didn't sound interested at all. Maggie and Tristan could both tell this.

Maggie leaned closer to the guttering flame of

the candle. "It's a very ssssexy book." The flame expired.

"My goodness, you blew out the flame on that one, Mrs. Welles. A sexy wildflower book?"

If he hadn't felt like a voyeur before, Tristan Mallory certainly did now. He stepped closer to the crack.

"All wildflowers are sssexy," Maggie said. Miss Roberts opened the book. Before her stroke, Maggie had been left-handed. Normally in right-hemispheric stroke victims speech is not affected, but if one were left-handed, as Maggie's neurologist so painstakingly explained, then speech is sometimes involved. In other words, she had thought, I am an all-around loser. I've lost my best hand and only tongue.

Using her right arm, Maggie lifted her left and slapped it on to the open book as a fishmonger might slap a fish on the scales. "It's good for something," she said. "Paperweight." Tristan smiled. How odd that so much of this woman's personality was coming through the wreckage. With her right hand she turned the pages until she got to the one she wanted. She then began to read. "Blood root: Thick; charged with a crimson juice. Leaves — rounded; deeply lobed. Flower — white . . . windflower or wood anemone or anemone quinquefolia. Stem — slender. Leaves — divided into delicate leaflets, flower solitary: white, pink, or purplish . . ." Maggie read on for several more minutes about white wildflowers. Then she stopped. Her speech had become remarkably clear. Her tongue no longer was a blade stirring thickly in her mouth. "You know what all these white flowers have in common aside from the color, Miss Roberts?"

"What?" And this time Miss Roberts seemed genuinely interested.

"They are all fertilized at night by night-flying insects. That is why they are white and smell so sweet."

With her good hand Maggie took off her sunglasses. There was an eye patch over her left eye. She had high prominent cheekbones and her right eye was slightly tilted upward and jade green. It glittered fiercely in the midday light. A breeze had sprung up stirring wisps of faded red hair around her head like licks of pale fire.

Tristan felt a little jump inside him. There was something ghostlike about her — ghosts of a sensuous being, ghosts of wildness.

CHAPTER 4

Martinis

In the traditional approach to The Moss Temple, one travels a path that moves through a series of carefully designed transition zones, leading from one "spiritual" world to the next . . . leaving the profane world of waiting taxis, teahouses, trinket shops and squid sellers.

JULIE MOIR MESSERVY,
Contemplative Gardens

Adams, Maggie could not help but observe, had the same ineffable grace as did his father when mixing a martini. Neither one of them was particularly graceful, or for that matter, well-coordinated in other aspects. Give them a lightbulb to screw in and they usually dropped and broke it in the process. Golf they managed despite having terrible form. Tennis eluded them entirely. Although they loved sailing, with their big feet and clumsiness they were a disaster on a boat. Dancing even the most sedate fox trot was a toe-bruising experience. But martinis! Well, all the dexterity and nimbleness of a Baryshnikov!

"Here you go, Mother! Just what the doctor ordered, I understand."

"He said one before dinner is fine," she spoke slowly but distinctly. The children were delighted with her progress. They had talked with the doctors and the therapists. If only they could start her moving about and out of the wheelchair.

"And he said a glass of wine with dinner was all right, too, Mom," Ceil chimed in.

"Never liked wine as a chaser for m-martinis."

Ceil smiled a taut little smile. "Well, I'm just having the Lillet. I find aperitifs are just fine for me."

She's lying, Maggie thought. She knew that Ceil went into the pantry and spiked her innocuous-sounding little aperitifs with vodka. There was a time, before her stroke, that she had been concerned about this. Being a lush was one thing, but a lying lush was quite another. If Ceil lied to her, she lied to her husband. And that wasn't good. But she honestly didn't care now. How could she care when so much thought had to go into every word she uttered, the simplest physical action? She now dragged up her left arm with her right. She liked to hold her drinks two-handed. Adams stood in front of her while she did this, waiting to hand her the martini. When this was accomplished and they had settled down, Adams cleared his throat and began to speak.

"Well, Mom, we've met your new neighbors."

"Wwwhat arggh they like?"

"Very nice . . ."

44

"A little bit flashy," Ceil interjected.

"Flashy . . . how?" Maggie asked.

"Well, you know, just . . ." She looked somewhat pained, and took a big swallow of her Lillet. "He wore a pinky ring."

"P . . . pinky ring?" Something wasn't quite clicking in her brain and it had nothing to do with the right hemisphere and an infarct. Pinky ring — sounded rather like something grown for Tussie Mussies, the old-fashioned Victorian bouquets. Maggie as a young girl had gone in the summers to Ireland to visit her grandmother who had a wonderful cottage garden and her Nan, as she called her, told her about Tussie Mussie flowers.

"You know, Mom, those rings people wear on their little fingers, their pinkies. His has diamonds."

"Oh." That was all she could think to say. Why should she care if a man wore a pinky ring or not? She supposed if he wore it to sleep and made love to his wife it might scratch. "Does it scratch his wife?" she asked.

"What?" both Ceil and Adams said at once. Since her stroke their mother often came out with these totally loopy non sequiturs. They were both thinking that at least this one wasn't overtly about sex or bodily functions.

"No, Mom." Adams clapped his hands together as if to announce that hard-a-lee they were about to tack and change direction in the conversation. He wanted to nip this one in the bud. Sometimes their mother came out with something pretty darned funny and then if they all started laughing and her tongue slipped out of her mouth and she bit it, there would be blood in the martini. "Uh, Bill Stein seems like a terrific guy. He's an investment banker, lot of money, lot of money! They've got this ritzy landscape fellow down here from New Hampshire. Does a lot of big homes, estates, worked for Rockefellers and the like. In any case, they're concerned about the wall. And well, Ceil and I . . ." He looked over at his sister and then they both turned toward their mother and smiled with the kind of bashful pride that children who have brought home a good report card might have. "Well, Ceil and I think that, even though this will go way beyond the yearly garden budget as stipulated in Dad's will . . ."

"Blow it, is what it will do. . . . Be right back, I just have to get something in the pantry." Ceil jumped up with her glass in hand. Maggie briefly thought she could call her daughter's bluff by saying offhandedly, "Oh, just leave your drink here." But it was very hard to speak in an off-handed manner with this paddle of a tongue.

Adams continued, "Ceil and I think you will be very pleased to know that we will put up the money for the repairs to your side of the wall."

Maggie felt her heart sink a bit. "Wwwwwww . . ." Adams leaned forward with a look of concern. Frame the thought, Maggie told herself: the crack filled with the blue — the man in the blue shirt and the silver hair, conducting the symphony of rocks — "Will the crack be f-fixed?"

"Which crack? There are so many, but I imagine so. I mean we're kicking in five hundred dollars."

Maggie felt a flood of relief. Her dear stupid children. They thought they were going to fix a wall with five hundred dollars. Five hundred dollars would probably barely cover the water damage at the base of the wall and foundation repair work. Perhaps they would never get to the crack. Ceil was back with her refurbished drink. It was at the same level as when she had left only slightly paler.

"Aren't you pleased, Mom?" Ceil settled into the wing chair. Kicking off her shoes, she tucked her feet up under her bottom. She now had a quiet yet effusive cheeriness — the bonhomie of an alcoholic with a refilled glass.

"Oh yes, yes . . . of course." But Maggie's thoughts had left the garden. She was looking at her daughter's nose. It looked red, and were those blisters? It appeared slightly corrugated. The women never got the lumps. She'd have to have Ceil's cousin Posey over. Posey was almost exactly Ceil's age. She wanted to compare noses.

The children were talking about something else now. Something about her walking and using the walker. "Elsie Lavin feels you're not trying hard enough. That you should be using the walker by now. And that by the end of the summer all you would need is a cane, if you really worked on it." This was Ceil speaking and then Adams interjecting. They went at it, a veritable two-person cheerleading squad/motivational team. "You can do it!" "We know that the old girl has plenty of kick in her still!" "Just put your mind to it."

When had they ever put their minds to anything? God, kids were annoying sometimes. "How about it, Mom? What do you say you give it — for lack of a better term — the old college try?" Adams barely got through Harvard and Ceil dropped out of B.U. after one semester. She, Maggie, was the only one who had made dean's list ever in this household and had graduated summa cum laude. Who were they to be telling her about college tries?

"Maggie and the fighting Irish!" Adams boomed. Oh shit, now they had her going to Notre Dame. She suddenly felt very tired. She turned to Ceil and despite her weariness spoke very clearly. "Go powder your nose. Leave the drink here." She adjusted her eye patch with her right hand.

<hr>

Tristan Mallory lay quietly in the bed of the guest cottage that was attached to the garage. This had been added in the first wave of renovations when the Steins had bought the house two years before. So extensive were these renovations that they had not moved in until three months before when the second wave had been completed. The garden design was the third wave. The Steins liked to have their "design chiefs," as Bill Stein called the architect of the house and Tristan, around when crucial stages of the work were going on. This had been their procedure when remodeling or building all of their numerous homes, which included apartments in New York and London, a place on Nantucket and another in Aspen. "None of this flying-in-and-out business. That's when miscommunication happens." It was a handsomely appointed guest cottage. Everything anyone could ever want, including a kitchen with a fridge stuffed with goodies made by their cook and a fully stocked bar. Television, stereo, Jacuzzi. Tasteful pictures on the wall and a shelf of good mysteries.

Bill Stein had discreetly suggested that if Tristan wanted to have visitors it was fine. His main goal was that Tristan be as happy and comfortable as possible for that is when "good work happens." It surprised Tristan that Stein talked in this way. For he had the feeling that the work investment bankers did, particularly men like Bill who bet against the yen and dealt in the strange mumbo-jumbo world of derivatives, was so abstract and removed from the very concrete nature of his own world of plants, soil, and design that ideas of "good work happening" just wouldn't occur to him. Bill Stein lived at the end of a tether of cellular phones. He was picked up in the mornings and dropped off by chauffeur-driven cars, not limos, but discreet black or pearl gray Lincoln Town Cars. He took private company jets and helicopters, rarely flying commercial. The first time he and Judith had come up to New Hampshire to talk to him, they had inquired about the nearest helipad.

Tristan could not fall asleep. He kept thinking about what he had seen through the crack in the wall, and the more he thought about it, the more awake he became. The woman and the garden in some ways ran together in his head. He recalled the moment when she had removed her sunglasses. She was a wreck, but when she took off her glasses and he saw her eyes, or rather her single unpatched eye, and the wind whipping her hair he had felt a quickening inside himself, a quickening somewhere in his diaphragm that he had not experienced in years — years and years. But it was resonant of something, some moment of transition, some moment of infinite mystery and charm from a very long time ago. The wind shifted. A sharp humusy smell drifted through the half-open window. Tristan remembered now. It had been almost fifty years ago. He was barely thirteen at the time. He was in a bog, a bog full of lady's slippers at the edge of a New England hardwood forest. He had been tramping through deep mud when suddenly he saw near a stand of ferns a bizarre and lovely wildflower. It was not in his guide book. And when he bent down to examine it more closely he was startled and excited to see its parts. Even though he was still a virgin and he had little knowledge of female anatomy, something stirred within him.

His eyes opened wide in the darkness now. He realized that he had felt that same feeling when he had looked through the crack in the wall and the woman had taken off her glasses. He never learned the name of the wildflower and he never saw one like it again. He had looked and looked in wildflower books.

Tristan loved in particular the Latin as well as the common names of wildflowers. They began to stream through his mind now like fragments from old dreams, dreams of collecting, or tromping through marshes and young woods — *Podophyllum peltatum, Saxifrages virginiensis*. And then there was the whole ginseng family. He yawned. How ironic it was that his first big job for Shreve and Coppitt, the Boston landscape firm that he worked for after graduate school, had indeed been the design of a wildflower sanctuary and that he was immediately yanked off that job and sent to Vietnam to basically redesign Phu Kat airbase and new bunkers for Tan Son Nhut in Saigon. Instead of *Calla palustris* and *Panax trifolus*, instead of mayapples and bearberry, it was C-141's and F-4 Phantoms with common names like Starlifter or Widowmaker or Thud. He had hated it. Hated every minute of it. Hated the fact that he knew as much about these machines of war and their specs, their requirements for landing and takeoff, for glide paths and wind shear tolerance, stall speeds and radar range as he knew about New England wildflowers. For nearly two years he had had to make regular trips to Vietnam. He found everything about the experience completely obscene. He hated the body bags piled up on the runways. He hated the way the officers tried to get him laid at the best whorehouses in Saigon. He hated the way the noncoms tried to sell him drugs. He hated the fucking air bases, the ugly planes, and the pilots with their pumped-up cockiness, and most of all he hated the chopper guys, especially the door gunners. Oddly enough, it was during those two years that Ellie and he were the closest. She seemed to understand in some tacit way his disappointment, his anguish. It was the best time for lovemaking during their entire marriage. For Tristan, their marriage was in some sense transmuted during this time into the sanctuary from which he had been ripped and sent to Vietnam. Ellie became pregnant twice. Their girls were born within fifteen months of each other. He thought of them as his own wildflowers.

CHAPTER 5

Parallel

To understand dry landscape gardening one must feel that the stones are living things like trees and shrubs.

KAZUHIKO FUKUDA,
*A Japanese Stone Garden —
How to Make Them and Enjoy Them*

"It's the most ridiculous thing I ever heard of. I mean really, why does Mom have to be so difficult about all this, Suzy?" Ceil was holding one end of the parallel bar apparatus that Maggie practiced her walking on.

"She likes it out here in the garden — rain or shine, she says."

"Well, it's definitely going to rain . . . watch that stone there in the path. We'll probably have to move this back in right away."

The two women were struggling with the apparatus down a lumpy path toward the most level spot they could find in the garden.

"I don't know what Elsie Lavin will think of this," Ceil muttered.

"She'll think it's great. She's wanted your

mom to get going on these parallel bars forever."

"But out here in the rain? You'll have to walk behind her carrying an umbrella. You'll look like one of those folks in India who walks behind the sultan and shades him." They settled the apparatus down near the garden wall where the path was the smoothest. "Now what'll happen is the goddamn wall will come crashing down and crush poor Mom to death."

"I thought they were going to repair it," Suzy said.

"They are but they haven't started yet."

"I'm going to run in and get a broom and try to sweep this clear so she'll have smooth going."

Tristan had to take the truck out to Waltham to get a decent load of loam and peat moss. The Arnold Arboretum was sending a fully grown Japanese maple tree, all twenty-five thousand dollars of it, and Tristan was not pleased with the quality of fill he had specially ordered to bed the creature down with. There were also several other big trees coming, including a magnolia and a dogwood. Their spots were prepared and he had enough good fill for them, although they were not as temperamental as the maple. There was no way he was going to unload the truck himself. He had hired some student help, in addition to Peter and Roger, for the heavy work involved in planting these big trees. The maple would provide a delicate screen through which to view the waterfall. Unless it was Niagara,

Tristan usually preferred glimpses of falling water. Vertical water and how one perceived it was very different from horizontal water in Tristan's mind. It had to be dealt with differently.

He had gotten into the habit in the last couple of days, since he had first seen her, of walking over to the crack in the wall when he had a bit of time on his hands. He doubted that she would be out today. It was raining, after all, lightly but raining. But still he walked up to the crack and braced his arm against the wall as he looked through. He recoiled immediately. He had practically stuck his nose right into the woman's face. She didn't seem to notice, she was concentrating so hard on what she was doing. It was indeed a strange sight on the other side. A parallel bar apparatus had been set up. At the end was a small staircase. Mrs. Welles, with an attendant both fore and aft, walked between the bars. The person behind her held an umbrella over her head. The person in front of her who was speaking softly coaxed her along. "Wonderful, Mrs. Welles, now when we get to the steps remember the little poem I taught you. . . . Okay and here we are." The woman began to softly chant a rhyme: "You can climb the stairs without going mad, up with the good and down with the bad."

Tristan held his breath as she approached the stairs and took her first step. She was taller than he had imagined. She was dressed in some sort of sweat suit. She did not wear a slicker like the others. He supposed it would impede movement. She was thin and of a very narrow build, although her shoulders seemed relatively broad. She was breathing heavily and there were little clouds of fog coming from her mouth. Her hair in the dampness fell in ringlets down her neck and around her ears. Through the gray mist she appeared soft and remote. She could have been a figure in an ancient Chinese hanging scroll. The crack in the wall framed her perfectly.

He had to admit that he was happy with the rain this week. Work on the wall could not get started. He was going to feel a bit wistful when they finally closed up this crack. When the Steins told him that the Welleses were only contributing five hundred dollars he nearly laughed out loud. But Bill told him to go ahead with whatever needed to be done. Bill said that he thought it was more the old lady's kids than herself who were the skinflints. The Steins would absorb the extra. It was a lot cheaper than being sued if the wall fell down and hurt someone.

Tristan had meant to go over and talk to Mrs. Welles directly when she was out in the garden, because even though they could not start immediately with the masonry, there was a lot of cutting back that needed to be done. The wild grapevine had been as tenacious as the climbing roses and had effectively torn out the mortar between the old faded bricks. That was another thing: he presumed that she would want to stick with the same tone of bricks on her side. It was a very nice look and Luigi had a good source. If he sandblasted them with a silicate mixture they really looked good. Very weathered and soft. He should go over there and talk to her, but something kept holding him back. There was something so enchanting about this distance. Was it the same notion that made him prefer views of falling water through the scrim of delicate leaves? He didn't know.

He watched for a few more minutes and then got back to the boys and testing the soil in the hole for the Japanese maple.

The sun finally came out the next day. Maggie was again in the garden with Elsie Lavin. "You are going to be on the walker by next week! Just look at you!"

But Maggie was not looking at herself. In fact, she had in that instant stopped in her tracks. "Elsie, g-good God, w-will you look at that!"

Elsie Lavin followed her patient's gaze. Trembling against the blue New England sky was a delicate embroidery of red leaves. A tree, a full-grown tree, was gliding magically through the air on the other side of the wall. "*Acer palmatum, osakazuki.*" Elsie looked alarmed. Was her patient speaking gibberish again? "Japanese cut-leaf m-maple — it's got to be fifteen feet tall. They b-bought a full-grown maple?" Maggie stared at Elsie as if she would have the answer. "I can't believe it. I never heard of such a th-thing."

"Wait, look what else is coming!" Elsie said. She was in front of Maggie and looking behind.

"Turn m-me around! Turn m-me around!" cried Maggie. "I want to see!"

"This is a wonderful time for you to learn this skill, Mrs. Welles. Now remember the rhyme. It's the same idea with turning around. 'You can turn without going mad, lead with the good foot, follow with the bad.' "

Maggie glared at the woman. "Screw the rhyme!"

She didn't remember any foot, good or bad. She just remembered willing herself around and then suddenly she was on the ground. There was an ugly shriek. She wasn't sure if it had come from her or Elsie. But it didn't matter. She was on her back and above her, floating across the sky, was a dogwood followed by a magnolia and a double white cherry tree — all full grown. It was a spectacle so rare, so magical, Maggie thought she had perhaps fallen through some sort of looking glass like Alice on her way to Wonderland.

"Are you all right? Oh, Mrs. Welles, why ever did you do that? Oh dear, I hope you haven't broken anything."

"Be quiet." Maggie looked up and watched the parade of trees.

"Oh my God. What happened? Is she all right?" A large shadow slid over her. Something blocked her view. "Are you all right?" She dimly remembered hearing a thud as if someone had dropped over the wall from the other side. It was the man in the blue shirt with the silver hair. He was kneeling down. His face was very close to hers. It was a most beautiful face. Deep-set intense blue eyes that sloped downward a bit. High intelligent forehead, thin nose, nicely angled jaw, and a very kind mouth. She had never thought of kind mouths before. She knew cruel mouths — thin-lipped, hard, tight little slashes. But the opposite, kind, was not necessarily fleshy and sensuous. No, this mouth was hardly fleshy, more on the small side than the large, but there was a gentleness. The silver hair was close cropped and the shape of his head was extraordinary. Perfect. Roman, she supposed. How else could one describe it? Could have been lopped off a statue, except it wasn't. It was instead attached to this man's body who was leaning over her and staring right into her eyes. She was glad she was not wearing her eye patch.

"I am fine," Maggie said quietly. "I am admiring the trees floating through the sky on the other side of the wall." She raised her good arm and pointed. "*Acer palmatum,* osakazuki, am I right?"

"Indeed you are." He moved to the side a little so as not to obscure her view.

"And look at that darling thing. *Styrax Japonicus.*" She pointed. "I simply adore Japanese snowbells but I never saw one that big. Must have cost a fortune."

"You bet." Tristan had been sitting and

61

looking up, but he could see that the view from flat on one's back would be extraordinary. So he lay down on the path. It was quite a show, he had to admit. It just happened that they had the extra crane there today, two cranes for the largest trees, plus the Bobcats allowed for quick installation of all the trees in one morning.

Elsie Lavin didn't know what to do. "I really think we should be getting you up, Mrs. Welles. The ground is cold and damp. It wouldn't do for you to come down with pneumonia now, would it?"

"I . . . I . . . I . . ." Tristan who was lying next to her turned his head and looked at her as she struggled with the word. She had a beautiful profile. She felt him looking at her. And took a deep breath. "It's the perfect place to be. I intend to stay here until the tree parade is over. There are more to come aren't there, Mr. . . . ."

"Tristan, just call me Tristan. Yes, we've got several double white cherries."

"Aahh, shades of Sss . . . ssss."

"Sissinghurst," Tristan offered.

"Exactly." She smiled sweetly at him.

"Mrs. Welles, we really must get you up. I can't leave you here like this."

"Why not? I'm so happy." Her voice, her words touched something so deep in Tristan that he could not even understand it. He just knew he wanted to be here next to her, watching the trees march across the sky. Listening to her soft hesitant voice speak the Latin names.

"Ah, *Prunus shirotae,* here she comes!"

"But I have to go," Elsie said in a whiny voice. "I just can't leave you here."

"Yes you can." Tristan got up. "Don't worry about a thing. I'll get her up and back to the house."

"Bbbbut . . . ," Elsie stammered. "You don't know how."

"How!" Maggie barked. "Elsie, this man moves trees, rocks — he's building a waterfall. It is a waterfall over there, isn't it?" She looked up at Tristan who stood above her. His face cracking into the loveliest smile. He had deep laugh lines around his eyes.

"Yeah. How'd you guess?"

"I'm not sure. I just knew. Now run along, Elsie. Any man who can do all that can certainly figure out how to move this old carcass. Oh God, I don't believe it, another double white cherry and it has to be fifteen feet high." Maggie was vaguely aware somewhere in the back of her battered brain that her tongue no longer felt heavy. That the words for the last few minutes had been coming so easily.

Elsie gave up. She walked away.

"Tell Suzy to bring my lunch out here." Tristan was now settling himself down beside her once more.

"Oh, look — another dogwood — how extraordinary. Full grown. Never heard of anything like it. How much does it cost? If you don't mind me asking."

"Not at all. Twenty-five thousand a shot roughly."

"Jesus, Joseph, and Mary!"

Tristan, who was lying right beside her on the path, turned his head suddenly. The thick voice was gone and it seemed to him that an Irish lilt had crept in from somewhere. "Are you Irish?"

"Born here. Charlestown. My parents both from over there. County Clare. I used to go back and visit my grandmother often."

"What's your name?"

"Oh how tttt," she stammered for the first time. Frame the thought, Maggie, she told herself. Frame the thought. But she barely could. She saw such concern and empathy in his eyes, not pity, just deep feeling. She pressed her lips together firmly. "Mmmmaggie," she said. "Maggie Flaherty Welles, and how terrible I never introduced myself."

"And I'm Tristan — Tristan Mallory." He reached over and shook her good hand.

That was how Suzy found them when she came out with the lunch tray.

CHAPTER 6

Night Stirrings

Deep within each of us lies a garden. An intensely personal place. Throughout most of our lives, this garden remains hidden from view save for brief glimpses during moments spent daydreaming or in quiet contemplation . . . but many of us long to make this imaginative garden real.

JULIE MOIR MESSERVY,
The Inward Garden

That night as Maggie lay in bed, she relived every moment of the extraordinary hour she and Tristan had spent together, first on the ground watching the lovely trees float by overhead, and then after Suzy came out with the lunch. When he helped her get up it wasn't at all the way the nurses and therapists did it. They always put their hands right under her armpits from behind and gave a quick upward thrust. He faced her and straddled her body, put his arms up to his elbows under her shoulders and then he scooped her up very gently, just as one scoops up a plant for transplanting. In one easy hydraulic-like mo-

tion she felt herself rising, roots and all, she remembered thinking. She got a funny feeling
deep in her belly when she recalled his arms
under her shoulders and the brief instance when
she was pressed against his chest. She had then
walked to the end of the parallel bars with him.
He was not in front of her the way Elsie always
did it, but in back, his arms on the bars, as well.
He was just inches from her. She could feel his
shirt against her back, his breath on the back of
her neck. The intimacy of the moment was overwhelming.

She needed to get out of bed. She wanted to sit
by the window of her bedroom. It was hot. A
breeze fluttered the curtains. The walker stood
by her bed. Since she had been practicing with
the parallel bars she had become much better
with the walker for short distances in the house.
She no longer had to ring for Mrs. Allen, the
night nurse. Indeed, she had spoken to Adams
about letting Mrs. Allen go. She did not particularly care for the woman and felt that Suzy was
all she needed these days. She moved toward the
window seat. She heard a scraping sound
coming from the garden. What could it be?
There was a half moon out but she could not see
where the sound came from, for it seemed to be
around the corner of the house, near the wall
where she had practiced walking.

On the night of her stroke there had been less
than a quarter moon out. She had been working
like a demon that day. The garden had seemed

all but lost to her. Two springs before there had been torrential rains which had wreaked havoc with the low stone retaining walls of the step gardens toward the rear of the main garden. She had actually tried to shore them up herself, moving wheelbarrow-loads of dirt and lifting twenty-pound stones.

Maggie's garden, which she and her mother and Monsignor John, from their old parish church in Charlestown, had originally laid out, was really a collection of subenclosures, or small garden rooms, through which one could stroll. But in the years since Adams had died, alternating bouts of drought with immense snowfalls in the winter had eaten away at the foundations. Erosion was terrible, plantings ran riot and then turned woody and brambly, and she did not have the budget to hire help for pruning and masonry. Last summer she had decided come hell or high water she would at least fix up the walls of the step gardens and perhaps throw in some bulbs. The gardens themselves were remarkably intact except for their walls. They had somehow managed to fend off the wall pepper and the snare of wild grapevines.

The work that day had been her undoing. She had begun to get a terrible headache late in the afternoon and attributed it to the hot sun beating down on her even though she had worn her hat. She had gone in for "a bit of a lie down" as her Nan used to say. She was feeling somewhat better when she realized that she had left her rings in a pot in one of the step gardens. She had taken them off because they did not feel comfortable in the new gardening gloves she had bought. It was about seven o'clock when she went out to retrieve them. She felt a little nauseous and dizzy when she got up but attributed it to the heat. Her headache, almost gone, was just a mild throbbing in her right temple.

She got to the step garden and felt a real wave of nausea and had to sit down right on the path. Her fingertips felt tingly. Suddenly the light began to drain out of the day. At first she thought it was an eclipse, but then she realized that the eclipse was within her own skull and that something very queer was happening in her brain. The European ginger that she had been weeding earlier blurred, then smeared. Soon she had only a pinprick of light through which to view the inky round leaves. She remembered seeing her left arm hanging limply and then doubting that it actually belonged to her. It didn't feel attached in the least. The last thing she remembered wanting to say had been *help*, but instead the word came out *piddle*. Then she fell over on the path.

She must have dozed off a bit because when she woke the stars were out and it was quite beautiful. She was strangely unpanicked until she realized that her left side was not working — at all. She tried to drag herself using her right arm, but she felt about as nimble as a turtle on its back. Then she looked up at the stars again and saw Orion's Belt and thought to herself, I guess I'm dying and it's not so bad. I have no pain. I am not even lonely. And that thought struck her as very odd, but suddenly she had this manic surge of happiness. She was in her garden and even though it looked like hell, this was exactly where she wanted to be. She had felt many times lonelier throughout her long, rather dull marriage to her loving but slightly glazed husband. She was at peace now. Someone would find her in the morning and it would be a very neat death, no fuss, no muss — nothing like that neighbor twenty years ago who blew his head off in his library and ruined a first edition of Henry David Thoreau and a Fitzhugh Lane painting.

It was a terrific disappointment to her when she realized that she was going to live. The cleaning lady found her in the morning and started shrieking to high heaven. Soon it was sirens and gurneys and people asking her stupid questions to which she gave even stupider answers. "Do you know where you are?" Of course she did. In a hospital. Mass General to be exact. But she answered, "Tobacco."

She was never in a coma or even really unconscious. There was just a fog around her for the first few days and when it began to lift, the anger set in. She realized that she had become imprisoned in her own body. Her tongue lay thick in her head and one eye darting about was making her see things double. Even now, eight months later, she still needed to wear an eye patch an hour in the morning and in the evening to impose a kind of obligatory rest, nap time for her left eye to keep the double vision at bay. She quickly became sick of the pirate jokes proffered by her children and relatives.

For the longest time she could never say what she meant. If they would ask did she want a glass of wine, she would say no often when she meant yes. Ceil was very good at interpreting this switching business. Ceil had been a dear in those early months, once coming to her rescue in the nick of time when the LPN had brought over her sister-in-law, a hairdresser, because they thought Maggie had agreed to have her hair cut. She had said yes when she meant no that time.

Maggie's hair was thick and still red, although faded with gray streaks. She wore it in a somewhat updated pompadour, but no one really knew how to fix it except Maggie. She pinned it with a barrette and silver combs that Adams had given her for their first anniversary. An occupational therapist had worked with her for hours. She could now more or less get the bun up there. Even so, her hair looked rather messy and slipped out of the bun and the combs until by the end of a morning half of it was hanging down her neck.

Rhonda, the occupational therapist, had come four days a week and put her through a series of skill-building exercises designed to increase her abilities for practical living. To accomplish this, Maggie was required to do impractical things like weaving on a child's loom or working twenty minutes a day with something called theraputty, the stroke victim's equivalent of Play-Doh.

But after months of occupational therapy her left arm just hung there limply. It was maddening. She had a secret name for her arm. Everyone, the doctors, the therapists kept telling her it would take a while and both Rhonda and Elsie claimed they felt muscle tone coming back when they kneaded and prodded it. They could stick pins in it, however, and she could barely feel the pricks. They had taught her how to use it effectively as a dead weight for anchoring things. They complimented her excessively on achieving this skill. Big deal! Maggie had wanted to say as she would flop her arm down on the page of a book to keep it open.

The anger she first felt at her condition had lessened, just as the doctors assured her children it would. But what neither the doctors nor her children knew was that Maggie suspected that although her life had appeared to change, these were just surface changes. She had begun to question if, in fact, the stroke had really changed her life that much, or had it underscored what really was a pre-existing condition, a pathology that had characterized her entire married life? Had she in some sense been in a state of paralysis for the past forty years without realizing it?

Had she learned to be a tacit accomplice to not just her husband's alcoholism, but as he sunk deeper into his own stupor, had she not become a real partner in the incremental retreat from the intimacy of a shared life? She had, in truth, learned to expect so little and not even miss it. Oh, it had never been that bad. No scenes. No accusations. Nothing "Irish" about it. Not like her Uncle Seamus, who was one of the most outrageous drunks ever. Uncle Seamus had never worked a day in his life and managed more than once to climb Breeds Hill in Charlestown where that stone phallus to patriotism, the Bunker Hill monument, scratched the sky; he would take off all his clothes, comment obstreperously about his own monument which had sired nine children, and then with it piss on the damn British. He usually did this on Evacuation Day, which in Boston was celebrated on the same day as St. Patrick's and commemorated the day the British troops left for good in 1776. The Welles form of alcoholism was so Waspy, so elegant, so controlled, and so deadening to every living thing that came in contact with it through marriage or work. There was something almost refreshing about Uncle Seamus now that Maggie thought of it.

So how had her life really changed that night in the garden? Not that much, she reflected now as she looked out the window at the dark garden in the moonlight. But today something had happened in the garden — so unexpected, as magical as the floating trees. She had felt things she simply had never felt. It was ludicrous — at her age and in her condition.

She had grown accustomed to the notion of herself both before and since the stroke as little better than her garden — a sort of carcass, quite dead but not yet fossilized — what with leaden arm and her entire left side weakened and with so little feeling. Her tongue heavy in her mouth. Words sometimes so hard to reach. And now after months of looking in the mirror at the battered wreckage, the detritus left in the wake of this hemorrhagic infarct that had torn through her brain like a blood-filled tsunami, a cataclysmic event that had until now only seemed to confirm a preexisting state of affairs — now, at last, everything had changed. The intimacy of that moment between the parallel bars flooded through her. She felt a stirring deep, deep in her belly as she had earlier in the day. She bit her lip lightly and looked out into the night. She could see the bones of the old garden, the one that she and her mother and Monsignor John had laid down almost forty years ago.

***

Tristan Mallory was sweating profusely. It was just before midnight. Luckily it was a clear sky with plenty of moonlight. He had in the last three hours dug up twenty feet of the gravel path where the parallel bars had been. It was relatively soft ground and he only dug three inches deep. He then had spread the sand to fill the path and smoothed it off. Now for the fun part, the stones. Luigi had overcut and there was just enough left over to pave a twenty-foot stretch. They would set fine for now in the sand and provide a much smoother walkway for Maggie. He had discovered two special stones. One with the fossil imprint of an ancient lily called a crinoid, and the other bearing a fossil of some sort of mollusk. This was why Tristan enjoyed working with rock so much. You split it open and treasures were revealed.

The notion of seashells on the tops of mountains had always entranced Tristan since he was a small child and his father had told him stories about how mountain ranges had risen from the seas. It was why he thought he was drawn to those tenth- through twelfth-century ancient Chinese landscape painters who painted on silk. Their landscapes suggested the constant intermingling through time of land and rock and sea. There was something so essentially timeless to their renderings. When Tristan had finally quit Shreve and Coppitt because he could not stand another trip to Vietnam and had set up his own firm, his first commission had been for the summer estate of a major collector of Asian art that put the Rockefellers' collection to shame. Tristan had fallen in love with a silk fan depicting a river with summer mist rising from it. The fan dated back to the time of the Northern Song dynasty in the eleventh century. He had managed to talk the woman out of what would have been a rather traditional perennial border into a winding herbaceous one based on the fan.

Through rock and pea gravel interplanted with ribbons of thyme and creeping junipers he created a "river" with "mist rising." The design appeared on the cover of *Horticultural Magazine* and made his name. Then every collector of Asian art and every museum that wanted a sculpture garden started calling Tristan Mallory and Associates. He was the youngest person ever to be made a fellow of the American Academy of Landscape Architects.

The clients he got through his work with rock, through his obvious overtures to Asian art, its paintings, even its porcelains, were very different from the Sissinghurst gang. They were all people with stories to tell. Their lives were full of narrative. Each one was in his or her own way, though they might not know it, whether rich or poor, a poet, a painter, an artist. Through carefully drawing out their stories, Tristan could make them appreciate themselves better. That was the most satisfying part of a job. There was always a moment with clients like this when a light seemed to go on and it was within that split second of illumination that they realized that, yes indeed, they had more than just money or unformed desire, they had a story and a degree of artistry.

Tristan might have felt a twinge of guilt about not singling out these two particular stones for the Steins, but then again, Judith had her heart set on a copy of a Verrocchio statue, the boy holding a dolphin, as the centerpiece for her stone terrace. Somehow naked cupids and fossils didn't mix in Tristan's mind. Or at least he rationalized it so. But it could definitely be said that Judith Stein was forever more Sissinghurst than Song Dynasty.

He would put the lily stone at the beginning of the walk and the mollusk at the top for Maggie when she had reached the summit. He set the stone with the lily and brushed it off, then flanked it with two smaller ones with jagged blue marks. The idea to do the walk had come to him while he had been having a beer just before dinner. He had not been able to get Maggie out of his mind. Since that afternoon he had been replaying every minute of the hour they had spent together. First lying beside her on the gravel path and watching the trees, hearing her soft slow voice. She had told him something curious as she recited the names of the trees and shrubs. She had said that it was how she spoke in the first month after her stroke — when she was not speaking gibberish or tangled sentences. She talked in formula, or she could recite nursery rhymes or songs, or parts of Latin from Mass, for apparently the speech center of the brain is located in a different region from the music center. Reciting the horticultural names was like singing, she said.

When he had helped her up she felt like a soft rag doll in his arms. Then he had walked behind her. It had taken them five minutes to reach the end of the parallel bars. There was something about her neck that he loved. He watched the stray wisps of hair licking down the nape. His hands were right behind hers on the parallel bars. The left hand was a dead weight at the end of a limp arm. It could not grip the bar really, it just dragged along with the momentum of her body. Toward the end of the walk she seemed tired and the left arm was having a harder time keeping up with the right. He could tell that it was important that they remain parallel for her balance. He slid his own left hand forward so that it touched hers and scooted it along. She stopped and turned to look at him over her shoulder. She smiled a lovely little crooked smile, and he basked in the light of the greenest eyes he had ever seen. In that moment he knew that he had fallen in love. He had fallen in love with Maggie Flaherty Welles, widow, stroke victim, Brattle Street dowager by way of Charlestown.

Tristan Mallory had been divorced for nearly thirty years. He had loved his wife, Ellie, but it wasn't long into their marriage that he realized that he was not in love with her. When he looked back, it never ceased to seem extraordinary to him that day in early June. Within the space of thirty-six hours he had graduated from college, been commissioned in the army, gotten married, and shipped off for Korea. Ellie had told him two days before she was pregnant. It never entered his mind not to marry her. But before she had announced her pregnancy it had never entered his mind to marry her, either. She miscarried about a month later when he was overseas.

When he came back he began his graduate work in landscape architecture and city planning. Then he had gone to work for Shreve and Coppitt. What he had viewed as the nadir of his landscaping career, laying out airbases in Vietnam, had become the high point of his marriage to Ellie. There had never exactly been passion, but Ellie in that time had offered him a refuge, a haven, yes, a sanctuary of sorts. But as his career swung into a higher gear, the intimacy they had found within that refuge seemed to seep out over the course of the next five years. As his practice flourished, Ellie began making increasing noises about feeling unfulfilled. It was hard for Tristan to understand this. She had seemed quite fulfilled before the children came. Had she found the role of refuge for him more satisfying than motherhood? It was baffling. He thought the little girls so extraordinary. He loved fatherhood. He was more lenient than she was, did not get so exercised over things as she did. He remembered that one of their biggest fights ever was over Barbie dolls. Ellie had become incensed. She didn't want her girls brainwashed with such images of womanhood. "Plastic and passive," she kept muttering. In Tristan's mind it was making too big of a deal out of it. It was at the moment a book or an object was forbidden that it acquired a new and irresistible allure — usually not commensurate with its worth. He had argued that she would never censor the children's reading as they grew up, so why would she begin now with toys? Somehow the argument got out of hand. All the baggage that he never knew Ellie was carrying about seemed to spill open, like suitcases busting their locks. She accused him of being attracted to her for her passivity; not only him but every male in her own family starting with her father and grandfather and brothers had celebrated women, valued them, for their passivity. Well, she wasn't going to end up like her mother. Tristan thought Ellie's mother was a perfectly nice woman. He was totally bewildered. "Are you saying that you are Barbie?" he finally asked, and then humorously added, "You sure don't look like her." The humor failed. She picked up a lamp and hurled it at him.

It was after the Barbie fight that Ellie decided to go back to college and get a teaching degree. Tristan was enthusiastic. She dropped out after two semesters. She then began a course of study that was more or less a patchwork quilt of workshops about the self and feeling fulfilled. Self-realization became her Holy Grail. One day Ellie came back from a workshop terribly excited. She had actually called beforehand to tell Tristan that she had some truly wonderful news.

The news was that she had slept with the workshop leader and that she had experienced her first real orgasm and she knew now that she loved Tristan more than ever and they could enter into a new phase of their marriage. She wanted him to have an affair with the leader's wife. It was not to be an affair of the heart apparently, just one of the penis. She had actually said, "This is not about love, it is not about emotions. It is about penises and vaginas. That's all."

That's all was right. Tristan was simultaneously furious and sickened. In a flash it came to him that for ten years he had been monumentally bored with Ellie and her self-absorption. He wanted out and he wanted custody of the girls. Ellie cried for two days and then took off for Aspen where she lived in a tipi for three months, until the cold weather came and by then she had conveniently met some man with a condo. Tristan had raised the girls in New Hampshire. He was very proud of his girls. One was a nurse and the other an elementary school teacher. They were good mothers and good wives and he loved them dearly, although he did not see enough of them. They both now lived in California.

The last time he had seen Ellie had been at Sissy's wedding. She looked rather waxen. He felt that she had had some sort of cosmetic surgery. This was true, but there was more. His daughter Ruthie, the nurse, told him after the wedding that she had arranged for Ellie to enter a drug rehab program. Both the girls had known for some time about their mother's drug problems and had, for some reason still obscure to him, wanted to protect Tristan from any knowledge of it. He couldn't understand it. He should be the one protecting them. But the girls were very protective of him. They had stopped introducing him to their friends' single moms some time ago. He seemed to want to keep that part of his life totally out of their sphere. He had relationships, but nothing of any real significance. He didn't seem to miss it.

But now, a twenty-foot walk down a path had revealed a world of intimacy and longing that he had never felt before in his life. He laid another stone. The moon slipped away entirely and he worked on through the night. An hour or so before dawn he finished. He stood up, his back ached and his knees felt numb. In the thin gray light of the ebbing night he surveyed his work. It was a beautiful walk. He had selected each stone so carefully and laid it so perfectly that in this light it looked like a gray satin ribbon. He could imagine continuing it to the rear of the property, making the grade transitions with horizontal granite splits.

He swept the walk clean of the sand, propped his broom against the wall, and then decided to take a stroll through the wreck of Maggie's garden. It was indeed everything he had imagined. There were the islets of ornamental grasses, now dried-out weed-ridden humps. And back in the southeast corner where the gray bark trees stood like Druids there was a moss-covered stone bench. The wall pepper was everywhere.

He could not resist snipping at it with the small Felco shears that he always carried in his belt. He soon realized this was ridiculous and went over to the Steins' and fetched the big loppers. By the time the sun was up there was a small mountain of wall pepper and brambles piled against the wall at the east side of the garden, the wall opposite the one shared with the Steins.

He wished he had not promised to fly with the Steins down to their home on Nantucket this morning. They were now thinking of buying an adjoining property and wanted him to check on the beach erosion activity and begin an initial site plan. They were staying over. He had planned to, also, but now decided to make an excuse for flying back. Even so he would not get back until early evening, and miss Maggie discovering her walk.

At 7:30 that morning the driver pulled up in the Lincoln Town Car to take them to Hanscom Field where the plane was waiting.

CHAPTER 7

Wick

The best paths have two characteristics: they lead to a point . . . where one can look back on the path already traveled, as well as ahead to the destination.

JULIE MOIR MESSERVY,
Contemplative Gardens

"We got to get you fed. Hope Fran isn't late. We got our bath yesterday afternoon. Suzy gave it to you, right?"

"Wrong." Mrs. Allen looked at Maggie in alarm. Oh God! Maggie thought that was the first time in a long time she had made a mistake like that, saying the opposite of the word she had intended. "No . . . no . . . no." She hesitated and looked confused. She was caught in a web of negatives when she actually wanted to say that yes, Suzy had given her a bath. She began again and drew out the words very slowly and carefully. It was as if she were preparing a little platform from which she could launch the correct response. "I had meant to say, Mrs. Allen, that yes, Suzy did give me a bath yesterday afternoon."

"All right, well, let's get breakfast down you." She took the spoon and began shoveling in the yogurt and sliced fruit that Maggie had nearly every morning for breakfast. She was not supposed to do this. Maggie was expected to try and feed herself with the specially adapted spoons and forks that the occupational therapist had taught her to use. But on the days Fran came, Mrs. Allen was always in a tremendous rush.

Maggie looked down at her left leg. During the day she wore a light brace. It was her left side that had been affected. This leg was thinner than her right one, with less feeling although not quite as bad as her arm. Fran, the other physical therapist, who came just one day a week now, would be arriving shortly after breakfast to begin the range-of-motion exercises for her left side. Maggie hated the days when Fran came. The exercises were exhausting and sometimes painful, but the worst part was that Mrs. Allen was always in a bad mood on these days because it delayed her getting out. She always rushed Maggie through breakfast and fussed about how she didn't feel it was right that Suzy came later on the days Fran came.

Mrs. Allen was indeed beginning to grate on Maggie and she wondered if there was not some way she could let her go. She made dinner, stayed through the night, and then made breakfast. That was the other dismal part of Mrs. Allen. If she had her way she would have given Maggie dinner at 4:30 and had her in bed by seven. She was always growling about how they had to start these activities so early because "You know, Mrs. Welles, how long it takes us to get you upstairs and bathed and into bed." Suzy was so much nicer than Mrs. Allen. If only Suzy could be her nighttime person, but she couldn't. She wondered again how long she would really need a nighttime person.

Twenty minutes later, Fran had arrived and the session had commenced. Fran had Maggie's flaccid arm raised and was ramming it into the shoulder. She called it compression. The point of the exercise was to send a signal to the brain to stimulate an impulse so that the shoulder would start to work. The problem with the arm, as they had explained to Maggie time and again, was that if it hung too long the shoulder joint literally let go. After ten minutes of work on the arm, Fran had Maggie down on a mat for a new series of range-of-movement exercises. Over the next hour every part of Maggie's body was shoved, pulled, stretched, and rotated. She was sweating by the time the range-of-motion exercises were over.

"Ready for some parallel bars work, Mrs. Welles?"

"Definitely."

Fran opened her eyes in surprise. Mrs. Welles had been very resistant to any work with the bars or the walker for that matter.

"I like to do it outside. That's what I did yesterday with Elsie. It's lovely. Suzy will help you move them out there." She couldn't wait. She wondered if Tristan would be working at the Steins this morning. Would there be more magic trees floating against the sky? Would he come over and see her? Maybe Suzy could help her with her hair. Good Lord, she was perspiring so hard she probably smelled.

Five minutes later, Suzy came rushing in from moving the bars. "Mrs. Welles, Mrs. Welles! You won't believe what's outside! You just won't believe it!"

"What is it, Suzy?"

Suzy's face was flushed with excitement. Her dark eyes danced. "Come see. It's got to be a surprise. I'm not going to tell you."

They wheeled her down the ramp that led out the kitchen door and into the garden. Rounding the rhododendron at the corner, Suzy said "okay" softly. Maggie leaned forward a bit in her wheelchair. She planted her right hand on the jellylike left knee. "Wzzat?" Her breath caught in her throat. Before her lay twenty feet of the most beautifully laid stone she had ever seen. And the garden itself seemed so much airier. Why look, she nearly exclaimed out loud — a clump of nodding onions, *Allium cernuum minor alba*. They rustled in a slice of morning shade. She hadn't seen them in three years. When they budded out they looked like a flotilla of small swans swimming through the shade with their long necks and bowed white heads. They had swum back!

But it was the walk that beckoned. It summoned. It coaxed. A weariness dissolved from her limbs. A sap stirred. "Wick," that was what Nan used to say. "It's wick." You nicked a dead-looking twig or branch with a small knife and you found a "greenish bit, something juicy" and you knew it was not dead. It was wick!

"Get me up!" Maggie ordered.

Suzy turned and reached for the walker. "Get yourself up," Suzy snapped. Fran pulled up her eyebrows in astonishment.

The commands Fran and Suzy sang out penetrated the wreck of a brain in Maggie's skull. "Reach with your good arm . . . set it . . . count to three . . . weight on your good leg . . . okay, count to three, take a deep breath . . . up!!!"

She could do this. She had done it last night when she had gotten herself out of bed and gone to the window. So this was the reason for the mysterious scraping sounds in the night.

She was up and straight and balanced within the arms of the walker. Suzy and Fran were screaming and cheering like maniacs. "Ohmigod! Elsie is going to be so jealous. She won't believe this!"

Maggie didn't even hear them. Like iron filings toward a magnet, she was being drawn to the stone walk. She felt his breath on the nape of her neck. She felt his hand nudging her own down the parallel bar. She suddenly felt her cheeks wet. Her vision blurred. And she tasted the salt of her tears as they coursed down the right side of her face.

"I'm here," she said quietly as she reached the stone walk. Suzy and Fran took away the walker. She set her hands on the parallel bars and looked down. It's a crinoid! she thought. He brought me a million-year-old lily. The fronds swam before her eyes.

Fran kept asking, "Who did this? Who did this?"

"No idea," Maggie replied.

But where was he? She heard sounds over the wall. Where was Tristan? Why wouldn't he be here? How could he do this and not be here? It was all so mysterious.

Up and down she walked, ten, twenty, thirty times.

Fran had left. Maggie never mentioned the fossils to either Fran or Suzy. She thought it was strange that they had not noticed them. Although her first instincts had been to point them out, she resisted. She was so thankful. It was like their secret. The knowledge of the fossils was theirs alone and somehow was resonant of the intimacy, the overwhelming intimacy that she had felt on their walk through the parallel bars.

He would come back, she knew this as certainly as she knew anything.

And a new kind of certainty also began to fill her mind. The world, her environment since her stroke could have best been characterized by a kind of randomness. Everything was transient.

Maggie had felt herself at the mercy of a kind of whimsy that bordered on cruelty. Now for the first time in months the world seemed anchored. She saw a direction and a plan. A plot began to formulate in her mind. She was no longer just framing words. She was framing something much greater. She was sequencing a course of action. The first step was knowing who was on your side and who wasn't: the good guys and the bad guys. Just at that moment the telephone rang. Suzy answered. "For you, Mrs. Welles. It's Ceil. Can you talk now?"

She wanted to say no. Just when one was getting the picture so clearly, framing up the good guys and the bad guys, a little reality check to remind you that the world is not that simple. Where the hell did Ceil fit into this scheme of good guys and bad guys? She hoped Suzy hadn't mentioned the walk to Ceil. She didn't want her becoming overly curious. She hated the idea of having to hide things from her children. She stopped herself short. What a lie that was! As she took the phone, Maggie realized for the first time that she loved the idea of secrets — secret parts of her mind, secret corners of her life — a secret walk created by a phantom stone mason. Of course, these weren't the kinds of secrets this family was accustomed to. They were into secreting vodka in their Lillet or pretending everything was just hunky-dory as their livers swelled and their noses became increasingly baroque. No, in general the purpose of the Welleses' secrets was to fool others as well as themselves. She didn't care so much about fooling others and, Lord, she hoped she was not fooling herself. She took the phone from Suzy and, putting her hand over the receiver, whispered, "I'm not going to say anything about the walk yet, Suzy." Suzy nodded.

"Hello Ceil, w-w-what's up?"

"Thought I'd drop by."

"I th-thought you and Gordon were going to that PBS fund-raiser."

"Oh, he had to work late and I didn't really want to go alone." When she went without Gordon she was sure to drink too much and driving home was out of the question. Maggie felt torn. She felt sorry for Ceil at home by herself. There had been several of these evenings recently where Gordon had cancelled an engagement at the last minute in order to work late. There certainly was a good possibility that Gordon had found someone sober and more attractive. She had always been quick to invite Ceil over. Now she had a sudden thought. Maybe Ceil could come over and give her a bath rather than Mrs. Allen. Instead of cocktail hour it would be bathtime. Give Ceil something concrete to do. "Well, why don't you come over and give me my bath instead of Mrs. Allen. I really hate that old bag." Ceil laughed.

This might be the next step in the sequence of action she was beginning to envision: getting rid of Mrs. Allen, who would be coming at 6:00. She would arrive full of intentions of getting Maggie fed and in bed by 7:30 or 8:45 at the very latest. Maggie had no such intentions. She was thinking about a bottle of Louis Jadot Beaujolais Village. Ceil might be a real help, but she still intended to keep her secret, even if she had to lie.

"Suzy," she called.

"Yes, Mrs. Welles?"

"Bbbbb-before you go." She was excited and although she had framed the thought her mouth couldn't keep pace. She took a deep breath. "Will you go down to the cellar and bring up a bottle of the Louis Jadot Beaujolais Village?" Suddenly the words slipped out with a new ease. She took another breath and the next sentence came smoothly as well. She almost didn't need the frame or the image. "Ceil's coming over to help me with my bath, but when Mrs. Allen arrives could you tell her that I want to have my dinner in the garden tonight and not until seven, all right?"

"Fine, Mrs. Welles. And since Ceil's going to give you your bath, I'll get dinner all fixed so all Mrs. Allen will have to do is warm it up. That should please her."

"Well, one never knows with Mrs. Allen, does one?"

Suzy grimaced. "I guess you're right on that."

"Oh, Mom, you are so much better at this than you were a month ago." Ceil was installing her mother into the shower and lowering her on to the stool. "I can tell by the way you are gripping my arm. Firmer, better balance."

"Well, it's about time," Maggie muttered. Funny, she had no compunction this evening about being naked in front of her daughter. Usually she felt a bit self-conscious about it.

"Okay, I'll hold the shower hose and you can scrub," Ceil said.

"Yes, I can now. Just hand me that sponge and squirt some soap on it. It's fixing my hair that gives me the most trouble, unless of course I have it cut off."

"Never, Mom! It's so beautiful — like copper."

"Unpolished — or rather un — burnished, as in dull."

"Come on, I'll help you with it."

"Would you, dear?" She caught herself just in time. She had been about to say she was expecting company. "I think I look as if I have a dead red squirrel on my head half the time."

"It's not dull. It's thick and lovely with the gray. Kind of like a sunset through clouds." Ceil raked her fingers through her mother's hair. They were both now looking into the dressing table mirror.

"You might think of writing romance novels, Ceil." They laughed. But she saw something in their dual reflections in the mirror that shocked her. Why did her mouth pull that way still? And Ceil suddenly looked so young. She had never felt there was much resemblance between them

96

but for an instant Ceil reminded Maggie of herself. When she had laughed just then all the bloat from her face had vanished. There were rounded childish contours. She could have been Maggie fifty years ago roller-skating down Warren Street, scabby knees, pigtails flying. But that self was gone. It seemed a cruel joke that through some odd conspiracy of optics, light, and laughter this image had been teased out of the mirror and settled upon the face of her alcoholic, bloated daughter. And to make it worse, the image was flanked by that of her strange, cackling mother whose face was split by a skeleton-like rictus.

She grew still as Ceil pinned up her hair. She wished she could close her eyes and not look at herself. Suddenly her secret seemed a little dingy. But the walk was out there. It was real. There was no doubt about it. Tristan had laid that walk. He would be back. She suddenly wanted to be alone. She wanted to look at herself in private. She wanted to try to believe in her secret.

"You should run along home now, dear. This has been a great help to me. You did a lovely job." She patted her hair but her eyes avoided the mirror this time.

"But it's so early, Mom."

"But Aunt Aldena is due to call."

"Aunt Aldena? She's coming here?"

"Well, if I can keep her talking on the phone it might forestall a visit." Maggie, of course, was lying through her teeth, but she knew that a sure-fire way to get rid of Ceil was to tell her that

Aldena was anywhere within a ten-block radius. Ceil hated Aunt Aldena with her nonstop chatter laced with put-downs and innuendo. Maggie didn't like her much better but found her more pathetic than annoying. She was married to Adams's brother Randall, a flagrant philanderer.

"Gee whiz, Mom, it seems to me that if you've had a stroke you should get a dispensation from seeing Aunt Aldena."

Maggie smiled slightly. There was a certain dearness to Ceil. She patted her hand. "I don't mind that much." She smiled again. The secret began to glow inside her again. She was growing more deceitful by the minute. "When you get older these things don't bother you so much." Like hell they don't, she thought. She was bored silly by Aldena.

"Okay, Mom." Ceil bent over and kissed her good-bye. "Anything you want me to tell Suzy on the way out?"

"No dear, everything is taken care of. Darling Mrs. Allen will be arriving momentarily."

As soon as she heard the door slam downstairs she turned and faced the mirror again. Did her face still droop a bit on the left side? Fran and Elsie had both said that the facial muscle and tone was back one hundred percent. Maggie wasn't so sure. She tried a small smile. It didn't look that bad. There had been a time a few months back when she felt as if her smile was sliding off the side of her face. But there was not even a pull to the left now. Using her right hand she brushed some rouge on her cheeks. She put a little pale green eye shadow on her lids — that always deepened them and somehow made them appear even greener.

She didn't believe in lipstick. She had always just used a natural gloss. It was too easy for redheads to appear painted, although she could hardly consider herself a redhead anymore. It was not as if she had a lot of gray, but on the other hand, it was not exactly the sunset through clouds Ceil had described. Somehow the gray that she did have muted the red. That's it, she thought, muted, faded. "I look rather ghostlike," she whispered at the mirror. She had a sudden odd thought: suppose she just faded away entirely, disappeared and the mirror was left vacant. Would that mean she was a vampire? Weren't vampires reflectionless? Mirrors appeared blank when confronted with a vampire. She laughed. Ah, there was a little color. Her eyes flashed green when she laughed. She wasn't quick enough to notice if that horrid little rictus split her face this time. Maybe she didn't care, but even so she had started to raise her hand to cover her mouth.

***

Tristan Mallory had one thought in his mind as the taxi wound through the traffic on Storrow Drive heading toward Cambridge from the airport: the nape of Maggie Welles's neck. As they approached the Larz Andersen bridge he noticed that light was leaking out of the sky at an alarming rate. Alarming not in any ordinary sense, but perhaps for a suitor of a stroke victim. She would undoubtedly be out of the garden. Should he knock on her door? Then he remembered a few days ago when she had been out there in the rain with the physical therapist walking through the parallel bars. What was a little darkness compared to that? But did the therapist stay after dark? Who in fact did take care of her at night? Could she get herself undressed and into bed? He felt a little surge of panic at the very thought.

⁂

"What!!" Mrs. Allen screeched.

One would have thought that Suzy had just told her they had beheaded a neighborhood child and Mrs. Welles wanted it roasted for dinner. "What, seven o'clock in the garden? This is getting out of hand!!"

Maggie had heard the first screech of Mrs. Allen and had dragged herself out of the chair in her dressing room and had negotiated the walker to the hallway. She could hear them arguing on the landing.

"I think she would really like it, Mrs. Allen. Really, is it that much trouble for her to eat in the garden? It's such a lovely evening."

"Trouble, yes as a matter of fact . . . you don't know . . . you . . ."

Maggie listened at the top of the stairs. She was sick of it. She would get rid of Mrs. Allen tonight if she had to. Suddenly something occurred to her and she should have thought of it weeks ago. The solution was simple. If she slept downstairs — and this would be easy enough because the couch in the library was a sleeper and folded out, and there was a full bath just off the library — everything would be simpler. So simple, in fact, she would never have need for Mrs. Allen again. Everything would be on one level. And wasn't that what they had all been worried about? Steps. The library tended to be cold in winter. She supposed that is why she had never thought of it until now. But spring was here and summer was coming.

Although the walker was not needed for the steps it apparently required a similar coordination, and it was felt the two — step climbing and the walker — were linked in this way. Since her stroke she had used the seat-a-lator that had been installed when she had returned from the hospital. It got her to the landing and from that point there were only three more stairs that Suzy or Mrs. Allen helped her with. "You can climb the stairs without going mad, up with the good and down with the bad." It was Mrs. Allen who was driving her mad — up with the good and yes, out with the bad.

"Suzy," Maggie called down.

"You there, Mrs. Welles?" There was surprise in Mrs. Allen's voice. No use pretending.

"I certainly am. Heard every word."

"Oh dear! Well, I just . . ." Both Mrs. Allen and

Suzy were up the stairs now, quite amazed to be greeted by Maggie in her walker.

Maggie had decided she was going to be clever about this. There was no way she was going to show her anger or tip off Mrs. Allen as to her ultimate plans for her. She didn't doubt for one minute that Mrs. Allen was capable of being one of those sadistic caretakers of elderly or invalid people. All sweetness and light to the relatives but proficient in executing excruciating but well-camouflaged acts of torture on her victim, not to mention running off with odd pieces of the silver.

"I am going to sleep in the library tonight," Maggie announced. "And shall continue to every night. It makes sense."

"It does?" Mrs. Allen had a slightly stricken look on her face. It was as if she sensed that her job might be in jeopardy.

"Yes, of course!" Suzy chimed in. "We should have thought of it before, but then again all your stuff is upstairs and . . . ."

"Never mind stuff, Suzy. I'll have a view of the garden — mess that it is — from the library that I find nonetheless very restoring. And now that I am better with the walker I want to be downstairs. You'll help me move tomorrow won't you, dear? And perhaps stay a few minutes extra to just get my bare necessities down for the night."

"Oh yes! I think it's a terrific idea."

"And Mrs. Allen, don . . . don . . . ." Maggie stammered. Frame the thought, but it was hard to frame the thought when one was lying. "Don't lie . . . I mean, don't fret . . . fret about serving me dinner out in the garden. I can eat right in the library and have a very nice view of the garden."

"But there's no place for me to sleep down here." Mrs. Allen said, a slight whine creeping into her voice.

Precisely, Maggie thought.

"I still have the call button. It works anyplace. If I need you I'll just push the button."

"But what about taking you potty in the middle of the night?"

God, she hated this woman. "I'll take myself potty," Maggie replied cheerfully. "The bathroom is actually closer here to where I sleep than upstairs."

"Well . . . I just don't know . . ." Mrs. Allen scratched her head. Maggie studied her. She had decided the first time she ever saw Mrs. Allen that except for her color, bright pink, she looked like a mud slide about to happen. She had innumerable accretions of flesh under her chin that slid into one another in neat, nearly geological formations — like sedimentary strata. Her eyes, dark little agates, could hardly be found within the matrix of pouches and folds. But they did seem to glare out with alarming intensity when she was crossed, as now. And her hair, which she permed religiously once every six weeks, hovered above her pink scalp like a pale, dirty yellow inversion cloud.

Suzy meanwhile had arrived with bedclothes in her arms. "I just can't believe what a fabulous

103

idea this is. Why we never thought of it before, I'll never know."

"I am not sure if it is a good idea at all. I think I should call Ceil or Adams," Mrs. Allen said.

Maggie and Suzy looked at Mrs. Allen, dumbstruck. Maggie felt something like panic welling up inside her. She must get rid of this woman but she must be calm and think. This woman was a tyrant, a real tyrant! Alter her domain, her sphere of influence, in the slightest and she felt personally threatened.

"I wouldn't do that if I were you," Maggie said suddenly.

"What are you talking about?" Mrs. Allen snapped back.

"Ceil and Adams approached me just the other day about replacing you."

"What? Why would they want to do a thing like that?"

"I don't really know. They feel they found someone better, but I'm not all that keen on it. I told them I don't need changes at this point in my life."

Mrs. Allen nodded as if this were an extremely sensible decision on Maggie's part. Maggie paused. "Don't you agree?" Mrs. Allen jerked her head up and down.

Maggie had a quick dinner in the library and an hour and a half later, a few minutes after Mrs. Allen had helped her to bed, Maggie heard a creak on the stairs just as she expected. "Just me," called Mrs. Allen, "forgot my knitting. Left it in the pantry." Maggie smiled to herself. There was always some excuse — either her knitting, or the *Herald*, or *TV Guide*. She had known for months that Mrs. Allen had been snitching booze from the pantry bar. She favored brandy and replenished it with water. She would switch drinks when the colors became too pale. She was not a vodka drinker, however. Lucky, or Ceil would have discovered her. When she came for Maggie for the midnight potty run, the Listerine was always heavy on her breath. Now she could tuck in for the night with her booze and the television. No need to set the alarm to get Maggie up for potty. Maggie could do it on her own, she assured her, and Mrs. Allen seemed genuinely happy about this as she contemplated a brandy-laced sleep in front of the television, which she rarely turned off once she was in bed in the guest room.

All was going according to plan and tomorrow she would contact David Webber, her attorney, and tell him to fire Mrs. Allen. Or rather Dave would tell Adams to fire her and Adams did whatever Dave told him, because Dave handled the purse strings of the family trusts and had more than once bailed Adams out of sticky financial situations. Neither one of her children was a genius in terms of handling money.

Maggie, although bedded down for the night, had not removed her sparsely applied makeup. She had asked Suzy to bring down some easy-to-pull-on pearl gray silk trousers, a white silk shirt, and her favorite shawl — a pale sea foam green cashmere. As soon as she heard Mrs. Allen start up the stairs she reached for the trousers, which she had asked Suzy to put at the end of her bed.

It took Maggie forty-five minutes to dress and she was exhausted after the ordeal and had to lie down for a few minutes. But it was still early. The sun had gone down maybe half an hour before, but it was not absolutely dark yet. She had put the bottle of wine in the basket of her walker.

From the moment she made the decision, hours before, about the Louis Jadot and the bath, she had never doubted that Tristan would come. The French doors from the library opened directly onto the terrace and then it was only an eight-foot walk to the ramp into the garden.

She was tired but happy when she reached the second terrace by the copper beech. She had asked Suzy to put out a chair and small table earlier when she had thought of having dinner there. She lowered herself into the chair. There was no way she could open the bottle of wine. It was all she could do to button her silk shirt, one of the few left without the Velcro fastenings, and putting on a bra had been simply too hard. It was odd, but in the semidarkness Maggie felt as if she were seeing the garden for the first time, or certainly in a way that was not revealed in the full light of day. The garden loomed gray and skeletal. There was a feeling of stillness, as if even the birds had abandoned it. Tangles of myrtle, wild grape, and ivy hung like immense cobwebs shrouding the trees. Although the *Acre sedum* had been cut away from the wall shared with the Steins, the facing wall of the garden sagged under the weight of wisteria. Climbing white roses had a stranglehold on the lattice arbor leading into the southeast corner of the garden. The arbor tilted at an alarming angle. The vines were so thick that there was only one little opening at the top — like the smile of a dead person, she thought. It made Maggie sad and uncomfortable.

Some years before under the copper beech, hadn't she planted trembling white masses of *Astilbe grandis?* What had happened? Stem rot? Leaf blotch? Aphids? Pallid mites? Crown rot, black rot? Tears began to roll down Maggie's cheeks. She was not even aware that along with her right eye her left eye, for the first time since her stroke, was crying, too.

CHAPTER 8

Night Gardening

By evening plants are refreshed. They are busy throughout the night as this is the time they make new growth. Nutrients which were manufactured in sunlight by day are mobilized in the dark and used to make new cells.

STEPHEN DALTON,
The Secret Life of a Garden

"Why are you crying, Maggie?"

"Oh . . . oh, dear . . ." She lifted her hand slowly toward her mouth. This was not how it was supposed to be. She had not even heard him. Oh, it was simply too ridiculous. Why had she ever let herself have these feelings? That he should see her this way! She felt so utterly stupid.

He stood in front of her and gently pulled her hand down from her face. A feeling of relief washed over her.

"I'm crying," she began slowly but the words came easily, "because under that copper beech there used to be masses of *Astilbe grandis,* and once that arbor over there that's encrusted with dead climbing roses looked like a piece of the

Milky Way come right down into my garden." She swallowed. "But I should not bother you with this. You laid that stone walk, didn't you? And cut away that small mountain of wall pepper?" She tipped her head in the direction of the pile against the far wall. He nodded.

"Thank you," she whispered.

"How did you get out here?" he asked.

"Walked — all by myself with the walker. You see what you've done? I've become an expert in one day with the walker. I went at least thirty times up and down the stone path you laid. Wore out the therapist." He smiled and she thought that even now the darkness could not quench the blue of his eyes. But better than the blueness were the deep lines that creased when he smiled. He was smiling. She had made those lines appear.

"Well, if you can walk, you can crawl, right?"

"What in the world are you talking about?"

"Look, there is still a load of wall pepper in this garden, Flaherty." He stopped short. She laughed. "I don't know why I called you that. You don't mind, do you?"

"No, not at all," she replied. "It's my name after all." Or was, she thought.

"Okay, I'll get some pruning shears. You go after the wall pepper over there by the peonies and I'll liberate the arbor from the dead wood in the climbing roses."

"Are you serious?"

"Of course I'm serious — cut away all this

dead stuff, there's a lot in this garden that is still alive."

"Wick," Maggie said.

"What's that?" he asked.

"Wick. It's a term that my Nan used to use when something had a bit of green in it, even though it appeared all old and brittle, nearly dead."

"Oh." He smiled again. "I like that. I like that a lot."

She could have probably done it on her own, but he helped lift her up from the chair into the walker. He had put his hands under her arms. His thumbs and the heels of his palms pressed into her breasts. She was certain he knew she was not wearing a bra. It gave her a lovely trembly feeling.

"You think this is a good idea?" he asked.

"What?" She was suddenly stricken with fear. Was he going to say she should go back to the house? That it was ridiculous, the two of them out in the garden at this hour?

"The walker — the ground might be uneven there. Would it be easier for you just to lean on me to get over there?"

Of course it would be easier and nicer, too, but she had to do it with the walker. Elsie said after three weeks with the walker, if she really worked on it, she could get by with a cane. "No," she replied. "Let's try it this way. You walk behind me. You can catch me if I stumble."

"I'll be right here."

113

Here — the word became charged with meaning. Distances between them suddenly contracted and they were again enveloped in a web of intimacy. Once more Maggie felt his shirt against her, his breath on the back of her neck. There was something so overwhelming. She wanted this single minute to stretch forever. But they were already at the peonies. "I'll go get some hand pruners." She wanted to call him back as he faded into the night.

She had begun clawing at the wall pepper with her good hand. Shallow rooted, it was easy to pull out. It had wound itself around the base of the peonies and was spiraling upward toward their heads. There was a fair number of fat buds that would blossom in another month or so. But the wall pepper would drag at them until they would stagger to the ground in defeat. The garish heads of the peonies made everything else look dim by comparison. She had loved these flowers.

"Here, try these." He dropped down on his knees beside her and handed her some needle-nose shears. "You can get at the parts near the stems with these and not damage anything."

"The peonies — you won't believe them. When they bloom I think of them like Las Vegas show girls. They're outrageous. One year there were three that had these huge pouffy heads — they looked like those peroxided blondes with the teased hair. I named them after the Gabor sisters. Zsa Zsa, Magda, and Eva."

Tristan looked at her and smiled. She had such a curious take on things. "Hey Flaherty, you missed some over there." He pointed with his shears toward some more wall pepper. Maggie dragged herself over on her knees.

There was something so satisfying about clearing away ugly dead debris and the rampant weeds that Maggie simply would not tire. She felt as if she were letting things in the garden breathe again and felt energized by the very effort. She discovered stars of Bethlehem and grape hyacinths gasping for breath under the tangled deadness. She and Tristan worked through the evening until close to midnight. Maggie crawled around, wrecking the knees in her silk pants and not even caring. They soon worked out a system. Tristan used the pruning shearers and loppers on the high stuff and Maggie attacked with the hand shears the lower dry and dead wood. He also brought her a clever little spade that she could start working around the roots of various things to stir the earth. He promised to bring over some 4-12-4 fertilizer and compost the next day.

"Well," he said, leaning back on his haunches along the woodland path that led to the step gardens, "I think this painted fern has a fighting chance now. I should bring you over some blue ridge phlox. It would look good here."

"I wonder if any of my old wildflowers survived back there." Maggie pointed with her spade to a spot just beyond where Tristan had suggested planting the phlox.

"Want to go look?" he asked.

"Gee, it's really off the path. I don't know if I could make it."

"Lean on me, Flaherty." He winked at her. It was like a current through her body. She was suddenly flooded with a sense of well being, of confidence.

"All right . . . all right. I'll try it."

Carefully, he scooped her up and tucked her arm under his so that she pressed tightly against his side. Her dull, insensate left side against his side. Even though she could not feel it entirely, there was a weight, a power. He was here. Again she wondered how such an ordinary, quotidian word suddenly brimmed with such magic. "I'll warn you right now," she said as they moved through tangles of wild grapevine and myrtle, "that there are no 'oooh la la' things like lady's slippers. Nothing of arresting beauty. I started it years ago with Monsignor John's help. We thought of it as the horticultural counterpart of the Greater Boston Catholic Charities — rescuing extreme cases. The first thing he brought were the seeds for Dutchman's breeches — one of the prettier things, actually. So fragile, though. We were rather dedicated to creating a haven for the 'little uglies,' as we used to call them." Tristan laughed softly.

"Hey, look ahead," Tristan said suddenly.

"Oh my goodness, *Polymnia canadensis*,"

116

Maggie whispered. On a stalk nearly six feet tall, a small flowered leafcup quivered in the night wind. They approached it silently. An unspectacular plant with washed out petals as small as a baby's fingernails, it bent in the evening breeze toward them. Maggie extended her right hand to touch it as one would the downy crown of a baby's head. "You should never have to be beautiful to be in a garden," she spoke softly. "There is always a place for character actors."

Tristan was watching Maggie now. She seemed hypnotized by the plant. She continued to speak softly in a barely audible whisper. "Well, with wildflowers, wild anything, I guess, there is not always a relationship between beauty and rarity." She felt Tristan pull her closer. And she did feel something in that dead side of hers. She turned her head slowly to look at him. He said nothing, but his eyes looked at her, studied her in a way no one ever had before. It was as if he were diving right down into her soul. Tristan himself was simply beyond words. He felt that he was in the presence of something so strangely powerful and extraordinary — that words, language, were utterly useless. He wanted only to submit himself completely to her rareness. But he saw beauty in this rareness, not perhaps the vividness of a lady's slipper in full flower. Maybe it was a light more than a color, pale green and shimmering like that found in the filtered light of a deep forest, falling in shafts piercing the leafy canopy and stirring the imagination.

They found a few more remnants of the old wildflowers but most had simply vanished. "I had, once upon a time, a sandplain gerardia, you know, *Agalinas acuta.*"

"Really!" Tristan was impressed. There were less than a dozen locations worldwide where it grew. "You know I used to go on collecting expeditions with the Society for the Preservation of American Wildflowers."

"You did? How much fun!"

"It was. I collected seeds of a gerardia once from a crevice in a limestone cliff."

"From a cliff?"

"Yep, in what we called a wind wedge where dirt and organic matter is blown and trapped. I think the gerardia liked the calcium of the limestone. You find a lot of good wild plants on limestone outcrop."

"But it must be hard getting them."

"It is. But I was their cliff collector. They always called me for those trips. I love rocks and in college I had done a lot of rock climbing." As they walked, Maggie imagined Tristan rappeling down a stone cliff, dangling against a deep blue sky, gently poking into wind wedges in his search for seeds of rare, perhaps dying breeds of wildflowers.

When they returned to the path, Maggie looked about. "There used to be an old damask rose back there at the beginning of the path. I think it's gone now. I like the idea of the colors fading, or a spectrum shift as you approached the step gardens."

Tristan had sensed that the step gardens, for one reason or another, were to Maggie the heart of the garden. He wasn't sure why. Perhaps there was no specific reason. With real gardeners — and he had no doubt after working these past hours with Maggie that she was anything but just that — there was usually one place where their soul and that of the garden's met. The step gardens were that place for her.

"Tired?" he asked.

"Not really. But you know I have a bottle of wine back there on the table. I was very stupid, though. I forgot the wineglasses."

"I'll get some."

"From the little house where you stay?"

"Yes. But first let me get you back to the terrace."

She leaned against him again as they made their way back to the peonies where they had begun the night gardening.

That was what they came to call it — night gardening. It was odd how their eyes seemed to adjust to the darkness. Tristan had brought a lantern and flashlights but they gradually abandoned them. Even when the moon was cloud covered it didn't seem to impede their work. So many things in the past year had been so difficult for Maggie but she now seemed to ply her way through the blue-gray darkness of these nocturnal borders with ease.

By the end of the first week they would clear out all the weeds and cut away most of the dead-wood. Maggie's silk pants would be permanently ruined so they became her gardening pants.

She had contacted David Webber the day after that first night of gardening about letting Mrs. Allen go. "Are you sure this is wise, Maggie?"

"I am. Please, I can't stand the old sot. You know she's a boozer. You should just take a look at the brandy bottle. If anything really happened to me she wouldn't be able to do a thing."

"But doesn't she . . . er . . ." Embarrassment seeped over the phone. She could imagine David's fair complexion turning bright red.

"Doesn't she help me pee? Is that what you were going to say?"

"Well . . . uh . . . yes . . . but . . ."

"Stop stammering, David. She used to help me but now I can get up in the middle of the night and take care of myself just fine. It's so much easier being downstairs. I don't know why I never thought of it before. Look, if it will make you happy I'll wear one of those Medic Alert bracelets."

Indeed, Maggie's progress had been so re-markable in the last week that it was hard to argue with her. The therapists all reported vast, astounding improvements not just in her walking and general motor skills but in her atti-tude. Her speech, though still slow, was never slurred and no more oddball mistakes.

The accretion of chins quivered as Mrs. Allen clutched in her hand the very generous parting bonus check. It was Friday. Her last day. Maggie and Tristan had been night gardening for almost a week now, and Maggie wished that Mrs. Allen would just get the hell out and not bother to thank her. She had a distinct feeling that the woman might go sloppy on her. The mud slide might begin to slip, part of some sort of excessive gesture of gratitude. The bonus check was way too generous. David Webber had said so himself and if Adams had found out he would have been upset. The single word slipped out from that drawstring mouth like a little worm.

"Tight."

Maggie leaned forward to hear better. "What?"

"Tight, I said. Your kind, the reason you're all so rich is you're tight with it."

Maggie was utterly dumbfounded. She lifted her hand to her mouth and shook her head. "I give you a check for three months' severance pay and you say I'm tight."

The dark agate eyes darted about behind the cobweb of creases and folds. "Oh, I'm not complaining, but it's just a tad skimpy. Jews I worked for did better."

Not since Maggie had been in the fifth grade at Holy Redeemer and was called a vile name on the playground by that snotty little Fiona Sullivan had she wanted to beat anybody up. But now she wanted to just beat the shit out of Mrs.

121

Allen. She wanted to think of the nastiest, meanest, most low-down name and call her that. She wanted to hurt her. She took a deep breath. "Just leave, Mrs. Allen. Just leave — right now."

It was almost miraculous. As soon as she heard the door slam the anger flooded from her. She never gave Mrs. Allen another thought. She was gone. That was all she knew and everything was fine. More than fine. It would be Maggie's first night alone.

"Don't worry about dinner, Suzy. A friend's dropping by with something for me. And it's getting too hot to cook. I love just eating fruit and yogurt in hot weather."

"How about I make you up some pasta? Then you can add stuff to it for pasta salad."

"That's an excellent idea."

They were on their way to the stone path to meet Elsie, who had arrived for the therapy session.

"Look what I found here," Elsie said. There was a flat of pansies of the most unusual colors — delicate shades but not quite pastels. Pale oranges, a pink the color of the inside of sea shells, a creamy yellow like the pages of old books. Maggie bit her lip lightly. "Oh, my goodness!" she said softly.

"Who could have done this?" Elsie asked.

But Suzy and Maggie said nothing.

Immediately after her therapy session, she planted the pansies. They would look perfect at the base of the arbor, now freed from the snare of the woody rose stems. Suzy walked with her to the arbor carrying the flat and offered to stay and help her plant them. Maggie, however, preferred to do it by herself. She said she would ring the little dinner bell she carried, for Suzy to help her up to the walker when she was ready. The very act of planting the flowers was somehow redolent of the intimacy of the hours she and Tristan shared together the previous night.

As she planted the pansies she reflected on the extraordinary turn her life had taken in such a short time. She contemplated this with wonder — a wonder that was thrilling, yet sad. Maggie had long ago realized that what she had felt for Adams was not really love at all. There had been, at one time, a true affection, but at the same time she had been swept along with the overwhelming enthusiasm of her family. That a girl from Charlestown should marry into one of the most revered and distinguished families of Boston was considered an astonishing, an absolutely breathtaking occurrence in life. It was beyond all reason and she had in fact proceeded, as she later realized, irrationally. People, of course, did this all the time. But how could she have missed so many clues — about his drinking, about his rather dull and undistinguished mind. And really, was what she wound up with so different from many marriages? She had never been profoundly unhappy. But now as she thought about it, what a waste. She had shared more in her few hours with Tristan than she had in a lifetime with Adams.

It was odd. She was not, on the day following their first night-gardening experience, impatient for the next night to come. That particular day was hot and the air hummed with the drone of flies and immense bumblebees. But the minutes slipped away at just the right pace. She could hear the men working on the other side of the wall. Occasionally she could hear Tristan's voice calling out an instruction. She knew he would not come over now, not during the daytime.

Through the crack in the wall, Tristan saw her planting the pansies. She was wearing a big straw hat that shaded her face. She was dressed in singularly unattractive Bermuda shorts and he could see that on her left leg there was a brace of some sort. She had finished planting the pansies and was now sitting very still simply looking at them. Her body was so different from the first time he had seen her two weeks before, slumped in the chair. She was still not sitting completely straight. But her body was not slumped, either. It seemed in a kind of graceful repose. She leaned forward a bit and touched the soil that she had just loosened with her spade. Then with her right hand she brushed over the pansy blossoms very lightly. It was one of the most beautiful and tender gestures Tristan had ever seen, and it seemed as if she had stroked him. The touch traveled to some mysterious recess in his own being. He felt himself drawing nearer to that place in the garden where its soul and Maggie's overlapped.

⁕

"I think you're remarkable, old girl!" Adams slapped Maggie's thigh and took a strong pull on his martini as they sat in the living room. Ceil smiled over the rim of her wineglass with her vodka-laced Lillet. Maggie was simultaneously bored and nervous. She wanted them to clear out quickly on this her first night without Mrs. Allen. She and Tristan had gardened together for five nights, almost a week. And each night offered a new surprise. She could not believe it, but along with the little ground-hugging bulbs like the scilla and grape hyacinths, some of her fritillaria had actually come back. Sprung up was more like it, after the wall pepper had been cleared. She was especially happy to see those old gems *Fritillaria michailowskyi,* with their diminutive garnet heads at the edge of a once-upon island of ornamental grasses she thought swamped or totally dead. She was expecting Tristan soon. But Adams and Ceil had called up and insisted on coming over for a drink. Cocktail hour with them could go on forever. Maggie suspected that their respective spouses had recently said something about their drinking.

Gordon, Ceil's husband, had approached his mother-in-law troubled by Ceil's drinking just before Maggie had her stroke. Maggie felt she was of very little help. What had she been able to

125

do with her own husband? Nothing. And Joan, Adams's wife, she doubted would ever come to her. Maggie was not sure if Joan really cared or not. She had the feeling that Joan had given up on Adams long ago. That perhaps was the main problem with Adams: he was easy to give up on. But Maggie never had, at least not while he was a boy, a growing youngster. There had been a problem with Adams in about the fifth or sixth grade. He had been caught stealing. It began as shoplifting and then he had begun to steal from his friends at his private school. Both Maggie and her husband were shocked and horrified. Adams Senior began to talk of military school. But Maggie said absolutely not. She could not for the life of her understand how military school would cure a thief.

"You're too easy on him, Mags," Adams Senior had said. "In military school there is a code of honor; it is part of the entire structure of the school."

"But we have a code of honor," Maggie had said and then it was as if a cold wind swept through her. Perhaps they did not have a code of honor, this old and venerable Boston family! But still, was military school the answer? Maggie had determined at that moment that whatever the family lacked she would provide for her son. She took him and Ceil on camping trips. Adams never went. He hated camping. She sent him on a three-week Outward Bound course in the Rockies. She practically single-handedly pulled him through algebra and calculus. There were numerous trips to Ireland. And although the stealing stopped and the grades somewhat improved, good enough for him to get into Harvard with a lot of family pull, she had the sense that Adams Jr. was receding from her in small increments at an accelerating pace. And then came the shocking realization.

It happened at the large family Christmas party during Adams's junior year in college. He had had too much to drink but the words nonetheless revealed volumes. "Lace curtains and two toilets — wasn't that it, Mother?" He was referring to Maggie's parents' house on Wallace Street in Charlestown. Maggie had looked at him steadily. Was this, yes she did believe it was, a declaration of sorts? "You mean," she had replied, "your grandparents Flahertys' home?" He snorted. "My grandparents Flaherty," he muttered disdainfully and turned away to get another drink.

That was when Maggie knew that some part of Adams absolutely hated her. And that part came from his own self-loathing and insecurities. It was why he had stolen and it was why, despite a genetic predisposition to alcoholism, he would drink. It would always in her mind be the real reason, more so than the genes. His father had never drunk out of hatred or insecurity but Adams would. He resented the fact that she was smart, that she could be Irish and smart and come from a three-decker with lace curtains and two toilets and be the one to pull him through algebra and calculus. But would she give up on him? Never. She couldn't. It made her love him all the more. Maybe it wasn't real love. Maybe it was some sort of strange addiction. Maybe she was a frustrated Saint Jude, the patron saint of lost causes, but she couldn't stop herself. She had brought this child into the world. It was her duty to make him fit, and she had succeeded to a certain degree. He never revealed to her again that flash of hatred. She had begun to think that it had dissipated. She felt that, indeed, since he got married and since his father had died he had grown to appreciate her in a more forthright and honest way. And now, ironically, she was not sure if she cared. Her Saint Jude days were over.

Right now as she sat in her living room with Adams and Ceil, Maggie got the distinct feeling that both her children were seeking refuge with her. She'd heard of children moving back in with their parents, but for God's sake, these children were forty and thirty-eight years old. They had children of their own. The children weren't home but in boarding school.

Was she being selfish? She really didn't want to think about Ceil and Adams and their problems. She resented being used in this way. Of course now they had the handy excuse that Mrs. Allen had been let go. She would need looking in on in the early evening.

"Are you sure, Mom, you don't want me to help you get ready for bed?"

128

Maggie was suddenly struck with how forlorn Ceil looked; not just forlorn; there was almost a barren quality to her. As she looked into her daughter's eyes she saw nothing. They reflected nothing. She looked at Adams. It was similar but somehow different. He did not seem so forlorn. The barrenness was more of a natural part of his makeup. But Ceil . . . Maggie wondered if Ceil had thought about anything but a vodka bottle and the level of the booze in her glass for years. Did she have any images in her mind at all?

Maggie thought of the verdant landscape that burgeoned now within her own imagination. Twenty, maybe thirty times a day she had thought of Tristan dangling against the deep blue sky; Tristan the cliff collector sliding his hand into wind wedges searching for the elusive seeds; Tristan scooping her up, her dull insensate side against his; Tristan and she lying on their backs watching the parade of blossoming full-grown trees against the sky; the walk down the stone path and his breath on her neck. And then there were the images of the hidden delights that were being revealed to her almost daily. She had actually dreamed of fritillaria last night. Great vast drifts of it — mission bells, in purple browns and whites and the ones called glauca goldilocks, soft yellow and low to the ground, or the spectacular persica, plum-colored, bell-shaped flowers on tall spikes. They might still all be there, just waiting to be liberated. For this was the season, early May, for these old and slightly odd members of the lily family. Suddenly Maggie was overwhelmed by guilt. She felt like a well-fed person in the face of a starving child. A millionaire in front of a pauper. But what could she do?

"Mom?" Ceil asked again. "Are you sure you don't want me to help you wash up?"

Maggie wanted to say, That is the last thing you need to do. She wanted to say, Are you sure I can't give you some of these pictures in my mind? I know a man who dangles from ropes in search of rare maverick breeds. I fall asleep with the image in my brain and the memory of his breath on my neck. As you sit here and drink your vodka I can feel in my bones a *Meleagris alba* nodding in the dusk. I know it's there. I can see it. But I can't give these pictures away. I don't want to share. I am a miser in my soul; I am a hoarder even when confronted by my own starving daughter. There are some things I cannot change.

"No, don't help me," Maggie said. "I must learn to do these things myself. Why, do you know today I was out there doing a bit of gardening and I was supposed to ring for Suzy to help lift me up to get into my walker but I did it all by myself!"

"Atta girl!" Adams slapped her thigh again and got up to fix himself another drink.

Would they never leave!

CHAPTER 9

Water

Don't wonder at foolish me for dallying with landscape gardens. It is merely that I use them as a device for sharpening the spiritual intuition.

MUSO KOKUSHI,
sixteenth-century
Japanese gardener priest

Ceil and Adams finally left. Maggie felt that she might have waved them off a little too eagerly when she stood at the front door. But they were gone, and with the first evening star Tristan appeared at the back door. She was dressed in the same dirty silk pants as the previous nights, a different shirt, however, that was looser. She didn't like to be braless under such a narrowly cut shirt. She felt that although her breasts were not huge, they were not exactly firm enough to go braless and still be considered attractive. At her age, shakes and jiggles might not be the best.

He was carrying a bottle of wine, and under his arm was a baguette of French bread still in its wrapper.

"Bread and wine!" Maggie said with delight.

"Yep, my turn this time. Actually there is a whole, cold chicken and some salad waiting on the terrace table."

"You cook and move trees?"

He laughed. "No, just move trees. I walked into Harvard Square and bought it all at that gourmet deli place. You're in your gardening clothes, I see."

"Yes. They're a mess, aren't they?"

"Just the knees. They become you, Flaherty."

She smiled again the little crooked smile that he had come to anticipate when she found something humorous or perhaps slightly embarrassing. He could tell that she was a woman who had not been able to enjoy a compliment entirely. She was not used to people paying attention to her in this manner. What kind of a husband had he been? A fool, most likely. The shirt covered her more than the one she had worn the previous evening, but he felt a stir in him when he thought of the softness he had felt when he had lifted her up and the heels of his palms had pressed against her breasts.

"You know what?" There was all the eagerness of a child in his voice. Maggie loved that.

"What?"

"We got the waterfall going."

"Really! Can I see it now?"

"Absolutely. We'll eat later." He held out his arm to her. She leaned on it. Then he tucked it closer to him so she fitted against him softly. As they walked into the Steins' yard she noticed some dwarf pear trees lined up against the garage that bordered the far side of the yard. "Oh, dear," Maggie sighed.

"What?" Tristan asked.

She pointed at the pear trees. "Mrs. Stein. She doesn't want you to espalier those, does she?"

"Afraid so." Tristan looked down at Maggie and smiled a bit. "You have a problem with that?"

She turned and looked up at him. "Of course I do. Nothing like nailing a perfectly nice tree to a wall! Horticulture's answer to crucifixion."

Tristan laughed. "You're something else, Flaherty."

"Well, I am Catholic. The imagery clings if not the conviction."

"I'm not Catholic but I can't say I like it much more. But she's got her mind set on it."

They walked on for a few more yards then turned the corner.

"Oh look, Tristan! That is just spectacular." They were approaching the end of the garden where less than two weeks before she had watched Tristan through the crack in the wall place the huge granite boulders. Threads of silver water cascaded behind the delicate scrim of red leaves provided by the immense Japanese maple. The water fell into descending pools graduating in size until the last of the three was almost ten feet in diameter.

"The kids can actually swim in this bottom

one, if they're ever here and not on Nantucket, during the hot weather. That's where they are now. First really warm weekend and they're gone." They were sitting on a stone bench by the pools. "Hey, Flaherty!" The blue eyes widened in a mixture of curiosity and delight. "You want to try something?"

"What?"

"You want to get those pants clean?"

"What? What are you talking about?" But he was already kicking off his shoes. She felt panic rising in her throat. He was actually bending over to undo her shoes. He stopped and looked up. His eyes had lost their brightness. They were soft, a nuance of a smile hovered at their corners.

"Don't worry, Maggie. We're not skinny-dipping. After all, the water might be cold, still May. We've got to wear our clothes!"

Maggie put her hand to her mouth and laughed.

The panic had receded but she was still nervous as she leaned against him and he led her to the water. Her body was not all that great clothed and dry, what would it be like wet with these silky things stuck to it? The leg as thin as a pencil, her stomach not exactly taut and smooth. She'd be like one of those old Fortuny pleated dresses come to life — or rather, not quite to life. And the old limp arm just hanging there and Jesus Christ, she wasn't wearing a bra. Not a pretty picture!

"Oh, T-t-t-tristan," she stammered, "I don't think this is a good idea."

"Yes, it is." He was now actually picking her up and walking to the edge of the pool.

"You're picking me up!"

"Oh, am I?" he teased as he walked with her.

"Bbbut, Tristan."

"You can't swim? Is that the problem?"

"No. I am an excellent swimmer as a matter of fact."

He was stepping into the water, then lowering her. She felt its coldness swirl around her. At first her clothes billowed out from her and then they began to plaster themselves against her. She felt his arms around her, yet barely supporting her. She saw her nipples perfectly through the wet silk of her shirt. "So what's the problem?" he whispered into her ear. She felt maybe the tip of his tongue on her earlobe. She turned toward him. Their faces inches apart. She cupped her hand around his ear and then pressed her mouth to it so the words would not escape.

"I'm ugly," she said in a barely audible whisper directly into his ear.

She was in his arms but floating. Now he put his mouth directly over her ear. "You are beautiful." He stuck his tongue in her ear and she felt a hot streak course right through her deep into her pelvis.

She looked down into the black water and spoke. "My left arm, it's a dead thing."

"Look at it now," Tristan said.

"What?"

"Look at your arm."

"It's floating!" Maggie said in complete bewilderment. She stirred it through the water.

"You're floating, Maggie."

"I'm floating? Oh my God, I am!" She began to move each limb, swirling them through the water. She rolled over and stretched out on her stomach and began to swim toward the screen of falling water. It was the most wonderful and delicious feeling in the world. In a few magical moments the bars of her imprisoned body simply dissolved. Tristan was standing waist deep in the water now, watching her swim with a look of jubilation. "What are you smiling at?" she called back.

"You!"

Nobody had ever smiled at her this way. Oh, perhaps Monsignor John when she had copped all the top awards at her high school graduation. But no, never quite like this. Tristan's wet shirt was molded so closely to his body that she could see the outlines of the swirls of dark hair on his chest. He sank back down into the water and swam toward her. They were close to the falling curtain of water. A fine mist sprayed their faces. He encircled her with his arms and Maggie lay back against him. "Look Tristan, look what I can do with my arm in water." She began to move it and her leg, too. "Why, look at this!" She marveled as her left leg rose miraculously in the water. "I wonder," she said as she watched her leg, "if there is a Catholic saint for buoyancy?" Tristan laughed softly. "You know in Gloucester — I went there once with Monsignor John for the blessing of the fishing fleet."

"Who is Monsignor John? You talked about him before, with the wildflowers."

"Oh, I'll tell you about him sometime," Maggie said vaguely. "But anyhow, at the Our Lady of the Good Voyage church, at the top of Portagee Hill in Gloucester, there are twin bell towers and between the bell towers is a statue of the Virgin. She has a bundle in her arms, but it's not the baby Jesus; it's a Gloucester fishing schooner. So there just might be a saint for buoyancy, too." Tristan smiled and hugged her tighter. "I should have done more water therapy I guess, but I hated the swimming pool where they took me and I hated the therapist."

"I'll be your therapist," Tristan chuckled.

"Never!" she said with a vehemence that startled Tristan. "You are . . ." she began but then stopped.

"What?" He turned her in his arm. They were kneeling in the water. It came to her now what he was. And he was definitely not a therapist nor was he Monsignor John. Dare she tell him?

Ever since Maggie had met Tristan Mallory, hovering in the back of her mind, on the edges of her consciousness there had been an image, a word or words that she could not quite bring into focus. But now she did. It was *gardener priest,* those monks of ancient Japan who designed many of the exquisite gardens that still lived and grew there. The foremost had been Muso Kokushi, designer of the Moss Temple of Saiho-ji and creator of the first *karesansui,* or dry gardens in which there is no water at all. It is only through the arrangements of rocks, pebbles, and moss that water is evoked in all of its moods and motion. There are references and suggestions of water — the swirls and cascades, still water or rippling ponds, even tumbling waterfalls but no actual water.

Tristan was her gardener priest but she could not say this to him right now.

"Follow me!" she whispered. She swam through the wall of water from the falls. They were screened now from the rest of the pool, the rest of the garden, in a cave made of falling water and mist. Two shadowy figures in a warm spring night. She felt Tristan's arms around her.

"You're not ugly, Maggie." She felt his hand on her waist. Suddenly she began to believe him. She parted her legs and felt swirls of water licking her thighs high up. She felt a lovely pressure in her pelvis and she moved her legs farther apart. She could imagine water reeds weaving between her thighs.

"Maybe not," she whispered.

"Maybe not," Tristan whispered in her ear and once more she felt his tongue, this time deep inside.

They were floating and whispering for what

seemed hours on the soft liquid billows behind the scrim of silver threads of water when Maggie's teeth began to chatter. They had not kissed. He had not touched her bare breasts. She had not told him that he was her gardener priest, nor had she told him the secret name for her arm.

CHAPTER 10

*Y*ugen

Enclosure of the whole garden is important to its sense of seclusion and gives even a large garden a degree of secrecy, so emotion builds along the journey. . . .

JULIE MOIR MESSERVY,
Contemplative Gardens

They never had eaten dinner that night. When Tristan brought her back to the house he offered to help her with her wet clothes, but she convinced him that it was no problem. She was, of course, used to arriving late at night drenched to the bone and peeling off sodden clothes! She doubted if she sounded convincing, but Tristan seemed to have an uncanny sense of her needs and her timing.

She did manage. It took her a while and she even got them into the clothes dryer in the utility room off the kitchen. She'd be damned if she would have Suzy discovering her wet duds.

Maggie thought that she would not be able to fall asleep, but she soon did and her sleep was laced with dreams of water, and always there was that delicious feeling of Tristan's tongue in her ear. And she dreamed of her legs parting in the water.

———✤———

"Oh!" she cried out loud on awakening the next morning. The tip of his tongue had seemed so real she thought for a moment he was there in the bed with her. "My God," she muttered. A dreadful feeling of embarrassment crept over her, then confusion. Had she dreamed everything? What was real and what was not? Had she actually been with Tristan in the waterfall pool of the Steins? God! It was all coming back to her in small pieces. He had cupped his hands over her breasts. But on top of the shirt. She was sure — pretty sure. But why? Why didn't he try to touch her skin? She could feel his tongue in her ear. She could feel the whispered words dropping in one by one — hot, moist. But what if she had dreamed up this whole thing? What if he just wanted to help an old lady get back on her feet, re-enter life, give her a little help with her garden? Was she a complete fool? She almost wished that he wouldn't come over this evening. Oh, God, she shuddered when she thought of how she must have looked in that wet shirt. There should be an alternative to confession for old silly Catholics who didn't really sin but just did profoundly embarrassing things.

But she knew he would come tonight. And it was really her turn to have something for dinner. Of course, whatever happened to that cold chicken he said he had brought last night? She didn't know how she would ever face him this evening. The morning proceeded at an absolutely agonizing pace, during which Maggie alternated between manic bouts of hysterical laughter and mortifying embarrassment when she thought about her soft, less than resilient, less than nubile boobs.

⚜

"Mom, how come you're blushing?"

"Oh . . . oh my goodness," Maggie said, gasping. "Ceil, where did you come from?"

"Well, through the door," Ceil replied as she walked into the sun room where Maggie was sitting.

"I didn't even hear you."

"Obviously not. You were sitting in here cackling away and turning bright red. I figure you're beyond hot flashes. What's so funny?"

Maggie started laughing hysterically. How could she ever tell her own daughter what she had been thinking about, what she had done? The wet shirt! For God's sake, the wet shirt!

"Mom . . . Mom," Ceil kept saying. "Mom, don't bite your tongue, remember last time . . . Mom . . ." But Maggie just laughed harder. Soon Ceil was laughing, too. They were laughing so hard they were crying and the shards of sunlight that streamed through the leaded glass swam crazily in the prisms of their tears.

They grabbed each other's hands and held them tightly. Ceil squeezed Maggie's hand, the

147

limp left one. The right hand Maggie pressed to her mouth to guard her tongue. "Why are we laughing?" Ceil gasped.

"I can't tell you." Maggie managed to choke the words out.

"Can't or won't?" asked Ceil.

Maggie sniffed. They had both begun to compose themselves. Ceil reached in her pocket for a handkerchief and handed it to her mother, who wiped the tears from her eyes and handed it back. "Won't," she finally said.

"Won't?" Ceil echoed, her voice full of curiosity. She raised an eyebrow.

"It's just too embarrassing."

"Mom! I'm your daughter, for God's sake."

"Yes, that makes it all the worse."

"But Mom!"

"Don't press me. Come on, Ceil, don't you have any secrets?"

As soon as the word was out Maggie realized what an awful thing she had said. A shadow slid across Ceil's face. She swallowed, looked down, then stood up and walked toward a window. It was as if something had shattered in the room. Ceil would never accuse her of anything, never get angry. That was not Ceil's style. She would simply clam up, retreat into that cold, lonely, barren place where she had lived now for years. Maggie wanted to say she was sorry but that would just make it worse.

"So why did you come by?" Maggie said weakly.

"Just to check in on you, Mom, that's all." Her voice had a little jumpy pulse in it. Maggie knew she was fighting the urge to ask for a drink. It was only eleven in the morning. Not even near lunchtime for Maggie yet. She could see Ceil's hands gripping the edge of the desk.

"That's very nice of you, Ceil. You worry too much about me."

There was so much left unsaid. She should worry more about her husband, Gordon. She should have more to do than stop by and look in on her mother. Ceil wasn't forty yet. She should be doing what other well-heeled young Cambridge–Boston matrons did — going to aerobics, or sitting on a charity board, or one of those book clubs. Every time Maggie turned around she was hearing about book clubs popping up where people got together and tried once and for all to read Proust. Mostly it was Proust, or some classic that they had never disciplined themselves to read. Didn't Ceil have anything to do?

At least Adams had to make a pretense of going to work at that brokerage firm. And Adams, she felt in some way had a natural inclination toward pretense. There were, in fact, a number of Brahmin-type institutions that aided and abetted such pretense to the point of delusion. Adams could always go and seek refuge, no questions asked, the Tavern Club or the Somerset Club, those special preserves downtown that represented the very heart of Boston male Brahmin society, those august sanctuaries of merchant princes, puritans, and gentlemen scholars. When men were separating from their wives, or were perhaps too drunk to drive home or maybe they were elderly bachelors who suddenly found themselves too poor to keep on living in the old family place that was falling down around their ears, they might take a modest room at one of these clubs. Come downstairs to the library and a black man in uniform would appear as if by magic with the requisite martini mixed just the way the frayed scion liked it.

Ceil had nothing like that in comparison. The women's clubs didn't function that way exactly. The women's clubs were actually dying out because all the young women had up and gotten themselves careers. What then did Ceil have? How could she, Maggie, a sixty-one-year-old hemiplegic, have more to look forward to than her own daughter who was more than twenty years younger? She wondered if Ceil and Gordon had much sex. She supposed if one was alcoholic it was better to be a female because erections would not be an issue. But if Ceil had sex, did she remember it?

"What are you staring at me for, Mom?"

"Oh, nothing dear . . . nothing at all." Maggie would have given anything to recapture the moment of just minutes before — Ceil holding her hands so tightly, both of them laughing like idiots. But the moment had evaporated, simply dissolved into nothingness. A silence stretched between them.

"I'm just going to the bathroom. Then I've got to go," Ceil said suddenly. She was going by way of the pantry. Maggie could hear the footsteps stop. If she tried very hard she would hear the cap being untwisted, and she would not even have to listen to know that Ceil was not using a glass. She would not do this to herself. This was Ceil's landscape, not hers. She closed her eyes. A spot of sunlight played across Maggie's face. She felt it. She saw the inside of her eyelids turn bright calico, then a jazzy neon paisley. She felt once more the pressure deep inside her when she had parted her legs in the pool, the imagined water reeds flicking high up between her thighs. She never even heard the front door slam shut.

By the end of the day she thought she was getting better. Getting a grip. She had only been telling herself to do that all afternoon, but at seven o'clock when Tristan showed up, she cursed herself for being a redhead. The hair might fade but not the capillary system that allowed this outrageous blushing that could better be called flaring. She felt it creeping up her throat. She could hardly look him in the eye. She began speaking almost immediately, barely giving Tristan a chance to say hello.

"You know, Tristan, there is still a heck of a lot of wall pepper around."

Heck of a lot. The words sounded odd. Not like Maggie. He smiled to himself. She's embarrassed about last night. It made her all the more

151

dear. He had tried to go very slowly. Go? Did he sound like a teenager, trying to get into some girl's pants? Now he found himself looking at his shoes and doing something with the toe of his boot in the ground. He had just wanted to make her feel beautiful. That was it really, wasn't it?

"Yes. It's still awfully thick in places," he replied without looking up.

"You know," Maggie continued, "over where the woodland path begins to dip, there used to be a wonderful carpet of pulmonaria. I had planted late-blooming lily-flowering tulips through them. It was quite something. I doubt if any of the tulips are left, but I have hopes for the pulmonaria. It's Mrs. Moon — that's the variety. One of the prettiest." She rattled on in a relatively rapid-fire style for her. He knew the place she was talking about. It was just before the step gardens. They began walking toward it, she on her walker, he beside her but not close. It was as if the screen of falling water had turned into an invisible glass wall now between them. They both mourned the distance, mourned the intimacy they had reveled in, which had now become something transient, a vagrant from some dreamworld, perhaps a complete chimera. They seemed slightly aghast at their newfound isolation.

The pulmonaria was salvageable, but the wall pepper had taken its toll. And there was one lily-flowering tulip standing alone in the center of it

152

all. A brittle net of wild grapevine had cascaded from a nearby tree ensnaring the tulip, the pulmonaria, and even the wall pepper. She and Tristan were working side by side on their hands and knees, their shoulders just inches apart. But still the invisible wall was there. Neither one of them could think of anything to say. The silence stretched uncomfortably. Finally Maggie broke it.

"You know," she began, "my therapist says this is the ideal position for my bad arm, leaning, that is, with all this weight on it. That's what she tries to do to me during therapy — jam it back into the socket."

"Why's that?"

"Oh, it's just that your shoulder starts to sort of come apart; the socket and the ball separate . . . and . . . and . . ." She sat back and rested, cradling the bad arm with the good arm. She would never know why she said what she did next. It was almost as if her tongue and mouth just went ahead with no consent from her brain. "Did I tell you that I have a secret name for it?" She felt as if she had suddenly become a bystander, an observer of her own voice, of the conversation that followed.

"For what?"

"For my bad arm."

"What do you call it?"

She began to chuckle. "You're the first person I've ever told."

"Well, come on tell me, Flaherty."

153

"Fishy!" And she flopped the arm up and down with her good arm. The glass wall shattered. They both started to laugh and then what hadn't happened in months suddenly did. Her tongue slipped out of her mouth at just the wrong second and suddenly there was a thread of blood trickling down Maggie's chin.

"Maggie, hang on a second."

"What's wrong?"

"You're bleeding a little bit."

She slapped her hand over her mouth. Her pupils seemed to dilate and freeze in a terrifying light of their own. It was that light of this terror rather than the blood that shocked Tristan. "Maggie!" he whispered. He reached up and gently pulled her hand down. She resisted. All she could think of was that terrible rictus that had split the face in the mirror. Like some creature from a horror movie she would turn into a skeleton before his very eyes. He wrapped his arm gently around her head so that it was in the crook of his elbow and drew her toward him. She felt his words on her cheek. "It's all right," he kept whispering. "Let me take a look."

"No! No!" she kept moaning, her hand still clamped over her mouth.

"What are you so afraid of? There was just a little blood."

How could she explain to him that it wasn't just the blood. "You're beautiful," he whispered. "You are rare and you are beautiful."

Maggie felt her hand drop into his as lightly as

a leaf. She looked up slowly and so afraid. He smiled a slow wonderful smile. "There's no blood now. There is just this lovely face that I want to hold and look at forever."

He held her face for a long time then drew it to him and began to kiss her. Maggie's first thought was that this was all so strange. Seconds before she had been awash in humiliation and terror. Now it had mysteriously vanished and been replaced with a deep yearning. She felt the pressure in her groin. She remembered the water between her legs from the night before, the sensation of reeds like ribbons between thighs. Then inside her mouth she felt his tongue. She was lying down now on the pine path. He was kissing her all over. He lifted his face briefly. There was a bit of blood on his chin, her blood, but there was nothing shocking about this. His hand reached under her shirt and he ran his fingertips lightly over her nipples. "Oh my God," Maggie muttered. His touch was like a match to her brain. They were on the woodland path by the bed of pulmonaria. It seemed exposed, too open.

"There's a place down the path in the first step garden. It's soft."

He picked her up in his arms and began to walk. Within a few feet there was a large flat stone set like a threshold in the middle of the path. It was, Tristan realized, a *fumi-ishi* stone and signaled an entry or the beginning of a

155

journey within the context of a Japanese garden. A white dogwood spread its blossoming branches like a small constellation over the path, which narrowed at this point. Stepping-stones appeared with wooly thyme flowing between them like calligraphy. To the left was a stone lantern. Tristan knew now that he was carrying Maggie along a classic *roji,* or dewy path, and it was the way into a garden, often a tea garden, that spiritually prepared the visitor. Mounds of moss began to rise on either side. The occasional trillium quivered in the evening, its white petals like a swirl of butterflies suspended in flight. There was a lushness that had survived despite the dereliction and decay of the rest of the garden. Directly ahead at the entrance to the first of the step gardens stood a stone basin filled with dirty rainwater. It held two bright red leaves that had floated down from the arch of Japanese maples.

The first garden was a sunken mossy room. Perfectly positioned off center of the moss enclosure was a pale gray rock, a *haku-un-seki* stone, to symbolize a cloud. Tristan knew that he was entering a place of dreams, a tapestry of dreams not unlike the Moss Temple of Saiho-ji in Japan. He kneeled and set Maggie down on the moss, then sat behind her so she was between his knees. He wrapped his arms around her and they both looked at the garden.

A slant of silver light fell through the lacy leaf canopy onto a Madonna lily. "I can't believe it," Maggie whispered.

"Can't believe what?"

"That lily there in the corner."

"The Madonna? It'll open in another couple of weeks."

"It's a miracle." The bells of the flowers were shut but showed a crack of glistening white. "I never expected it to make it here — so much shade. It was a gamble planting it here."

"They're tough."

"But . . ." Maggie looked around the garden slowly. Her eyes were becoming accustomed to the darkness. Other things began to separate themselves from the night. Around the base of the *haku-un-seki* stone she could see a fleeting tapestry of snowdrops and grape hyacinths. Were the bulbs as astonished to see her as she was to see them? "I . . . I just never expected . . ." She broke off the thought again. She turned and looked at Tristan. "You know, this is where it happened?"

"What happened?"

"The queerness in . . ." She began again. "My stroke," she said softly, then continued. "I had planted the Madonna lily in the morning. I had worked on the walls in the afternoon. When I had started to feel sick . . . well, at first it was just my stomach and this terrible headache. I was trying to plant some more bulbs. So many of the muscari and the snowdrops had died out I had bought some more. But my hands weren't working right, nor my eyes, and I could hardly dig. I'm sure I planted them much too shallow.

157

Maybe even upside down. Everything had become so queer. But they're here."

"And so are you," Tristan said and stroked her cheek.

Maggie smiled ever so slightly. "Yes," she said softly, "and you, too."

He moved back and lowered her onto the moss. He kneeled over her and kissed her again. She felt his hand on her rib cage. She felt her heart beating so loud, so insistently that she thought it might make his hand jump up, but then both his hands began moving down toward her waist. He slid down the silk gardening trousers and then her underpants. She felt the moss against her skin while she waited for him to open his own trousers. Then he entered her.

He could feel her trying to rise to meet his thrust and the very effort excited him more. He slid his hand under her bottom and lifted her toward him. He would carry her into him and himself into her. He would lift her to the sky if he had to. And Maggie felt herself swept away. She looked up and saw behind the lace of the leaves to the stars in the liquid night. She could feel the snowdrops trembling a few feet away. The Madonna lily opened a fraction of a millimeter and Maggie herself seemed to flow and become part of all the growing things around her. It was not just as if her body had returned to her, but it had returned nearly unrecognizable, stretching with yearning and brimming wetness. There were crevices of pleasure that had forever been hidden until these moments. She who had not had sex in nearly fifteen years swelled with pleasure inside as she magically rose to meet his thrusts. She felt an orgasm start to build. It began and it went on and on and on as Maggie rocked on the mossy bed.

When they were finished, Tristan gently moved off her and they looked into each other's eyes for a long time and said nothing. A leaf from a Japanese maple drifted down lazily and settled on Maggie's belly just beneath her navel like some silent benediction. Tristan cupped his hand over her soft fur and kissed her. Then he began moving down her body. She felt the melting sensation begin again. He kissed her and gave her little nips all down the left side, which still was dull in comparison to her right side. He mouthed the limp left arm and sucked on the nipple of her left breast and then moved down, down until he came to the leaf. He picked it up.

"Move your legs apart. Let them fall open."

She slid the right leg over. The left remained where it was. He lifted the left leg just above the brace and moved it. He took the maple leaf and brushed the inside of her thigh, reaching higher and higher to the moist petals. She moaned with pleasure. She thought of foxglove in the morning, the pink throats glistening with dew. He took his fingers and spread the lips and then tickled her inside. "Be in me again, Tristan. Please God! Come into me again!"

He kicked his trousers aside and stood over

her, straddling her. Once more he scooped her up under her arms as he had the first time he had lifted her. "What are you doing?" she whispered.

"Can you just stay on your knees a minute?"

"Yes."

He then lay down on his back. "Come here, Flaherty," he said, holding out his arms. He embraced her and pulled her toward him. She saw what he wanted her to do. She struggled to get her right leg over him. They began laughing. He reached for the left leg and dragged it close to his side. Soon she was sitting astride him, but too high up on his chest. She looked over her shoulder and saw his penis immense in the darkness.

"You gotta get there." He laughed and scooted himself back so that she slid down on his belly. She felt it now, warm and wet against the small of her back. Tristan slid his hands under her thighs and lifted her slightly. Then she felt it between her legs, so hard. He took it in his hand and soon he was inside her again.

"Now I'll do all the work and you just ride!"

Maggie rose in the night as he pushed his hips upward. She looked down at him and smiled broadly, widely. She didn't care if her face pulled or her smile slid right off her chin. And as he pushed into her she noticed new things in the garden pushing through the moss. The fierce green points of late spring bulbs that she had planted to lighten up the shadiest corners. They were all working their way to the surface, struggling with all their might, their roots tangled and mysteriously deep within the earth. She looked straight down at their pelvises working against each other. Glimpses of wet pink midst tangles of hair. He was growing bigger inside of her. She felt it. Filling her.

He felt bell song, a narcissus, was Maggie's color in terms of sex. Her thin pubic hair, which had probably at one time been an intense auburn, was now this same faded pink-orange of the narcissus cup. These colors, the intense flash of her green eyes and the slight movement of her breasts that hung above him like swaying moons drew him closer to the center of some ancient erotic conspiracy. He felt himself begin to come.

The mossy space within the step garden seemed to alternately recede and contract. In one moment Tristan felt huge in a small womblike world and in the next he felt himself engulfed by the immensity of the night. He knew in a sense this was the enigma at the heart of every true Japanese garden — one's sense of scale was knocked off; one was no longer the size he thought, neither spiritually nor physically. He felt alternately immense and minute. Just before he came he had looked over Maggie's shoulder as she rose and fell like an entire ocean on him, and caught sight of the garden beyond — the second step garden that seemed to overlap for a brief instant with the one he was in, creating an uncertainty as to the depth of field; an illusion of depth.

This was a Japanese gardening strategy called *shakkei*. The low stone, moss-encrusted wall of this garden had a notch in its center that framed the rock in the garden below. The simple rock, which might not have been more than a foot high, suddenly loomed like a mountain in a vast yet only partially revealed landscape. It was all part of Maggie's original composition for the step gardens. And through this composition Maggie was bringing him closer to the secret that the great ancient gardener priests of Japan were always approaching. They called it *yugen* and it meant tranquility, stillness in movement, the eternity within the transient. It meant mystery and depth.

After he came and Maggie lay on top of him folded in his arms he whispered in her ear, "Have you ever heard the word *yugen*, Maggie?"

"Yes," she whispered back.

"There was an ancient Japanese monk. He lived in the fifteenth century. His name was Shotetsu and he once said that *yugen* can be the thin cloud veiling the moon or the autumn mist wrapping the scarlet leaves on a mountainside."

"Or the reflection of a flower's color in a dew drop at dawn," Maggie whispered.

"Yes," he said and stroked the small of her back. So he knows, Maggie thought. He knows what he is to me and I never have to say the words.

Yugen also meant the lingering resonance of passing things and they both knew that come what may, they might, when they possessed nothing, possess all — if they were lucky. And this was the paradox of life, the riddle of a Japanese garden.

After midnight, Tristan carried Maggie back to her house. He bathed her and then climbed into bed next to her. In the gray light of the dawn he left. She stirred. He kissed her. She mumbled something about how it wouldn't do for Suzy to find him there.

She went back to sleep. She had no dreams. She slept soundly until she heard the key in the front door.

There had been two witnesses that first night to Maggie's and Tristan's lovemaking in the step garden. Maggie had noticed the first one when Tristan had slid his hands under her and lifted her hips to meet him. There had been a wonderful spiderweb strung in the branches of the Japanese maple. The moon illuminated the silver geometry of the web and she had spotted the spider on one of the radials. The second witness was a green laced-wing fly that lighted down for a brief instant on the trembling *Astilbe grandis*.

Maggie liked to think of them as witnesses. That week the weather was warm and clear and every night they returned to the step garden and new nocturnal witnesses swept through while they were making love. It made Maggie happy, for she had thought just a week before that the garden had been abandoned by everything — even the birds. But they were there. A garrulous jay flew right over them as Maggie astride Tristan threw her head back to sigh into the night with her pleasure. When the moon was full she could spot them all — the snail along the stone wall, a moth the color of a canary, a swooping bat carving arcs in the night.

The second week it rained quite a bit and Tristan had work on the North Shore of Boston, a project in Manchester, and then he had to go down to Nantucket for the Steins. Maggie had given him a key to the back door and when he would return, often late, he would slip into bed beside her. They would make love once when he first got there and then once more in the pale gray light of the dawn. He would leave before Suzy arrived.

By late May, the dogwood had gone by, and the one that marked the beginning of the *roji* path was in full leaf. Tristan had said it was quite remarkable that it had not been attacked by the borers that were killing so many of the American dogwoods. He did, however, spray it for Maggie as a "prophylactic" measure.

"Isn't it wonderful," Maggie said, "that we don't have to worry about that?" They were in bed and it was raining softly outside.

"What?" Tristan said.

"Getting pregnant. You didn't think I meant

getting borers, did you?"

"That's how I got married the first time," Tristan said.

"No! Really?"

"Yes. I was dumb."

"Well, it takes two."

"I suppose it does. Did you have sex with your husband before you were married?"

"Once."

"Just once?"

"Yes, I didn't think it was worth having to go to confession about."

Tristan laughed hard at this. "Wasn't all you expected, huh?"

"Well, underwhelming to say the least. I was a virgin. Adams and I were engaged. Adams was slightly tipsy at the time. He thought that was why it hadn't worked so well for me. And maybe it was. But after we were married, well, he actually had problems in the first years of our marriage if he hadn't had something to drink and then at the end if he had. It was rather a damned-if-you-do, damned-if-you-don't situation."

"Gee, that doesn't sound so great."

"It wasn't so bad. You know I didn't know quite what it could be until now." He leaned over and kissed her neck.

"And now . . ." Her voice was growing husky.

"Now what?"

"I can't get enough of you." She laughed. "Am I turning into a sixty-one-year-old nymphomaniac?"

"You mean a dirty old lady?" Tristan was on top of her.

"Oh, I like that. I like that a lot. There is nothing better than being a dirty old lady, especially when you're Roman Catholic and Irish and you're the widow of a descendant of John Quincy Adams." They kept their eyes wide open and drank in each other's being with all they could.

***

By Memorial Day weekend, the Steins had gone to Nantucket for more or less the rest of the summer. "What a shame, to go now!" Maggie said as she walked through their garden on Tristan's arm. "It's so beautiful. I'd kill for these late-blooming tulips. As you see, mine are gone. You know, here in Cambridge between the squirrel population and the shade it's really hard to have them carry over from year to year."

"Yeah, I came down early last fall and grubbed out a few areas for the bulbs before we really began on the rest of the garden. She wanted them and now here they're in bloom, and the Steins up and go to Nantucket. People that rich are kind of funny."

"I guess."

"They don't exactly live in their houses. They are sort of like stage managers for scenes that happen in them. Judith Stein is on a continual search for real estate. They have an apartment in New York — thank God nothing for me to landscape there. They have a house in Aspen. But then there's also talk of one in Santa Fe . . . all the hot spots. Desert gardening can be interesting. It's a whole other palette of color and range of textures you're dealing with. And then the light. I have another client out there now. "

"Hey, Mom! What ya doing over there?"
"Oh dear God!" muttered Maggie.

Over the wall, floating like a strange balloon, Tristan saw an immense pink face. The fellow must have been standing on the ladder that Peter had left when he had begun preparing the crack in the wall for Luigi to repair.
"Oh, Adams! What a surprise."
This was Maggie's son? Tristan couldn't believe it. The guy looked old enough to be her brother, and not a younger one. Maggie had told him very little about her children except to hint at the fact they had the same drinking problems as her husband. He knew that her kids were somewhat older than his and nearing forty, but this guy looked over fifty.
"We better go back," she said tensely.
Her hand gripped Tristan's arm like a claw. Speech seemed to vanish.

Frame it! Frame it! For the first time in weeks Maggie could not make the words. Letters, sounds, fragments of words floated around in her brain willy-nilly. *I want* came close to coming out as *marigold*. She knew what she wanted to do:

introduce Tristan to Adams. But for the life of her she couldn't grasp the words. They flew by her at first like butterflies, taunting her with a brilliance they did not deserve. And then no butterflies at all, but dull, dun-colored moths in the endless night of her growing aphasia. Simple words escaped her, colorless words like *This is Mr. Mallory . . . he is the landscape architect for the Steins . . . this is my son Adams. . . .*

But Adams did not look good. He never looked great. His nose had taken on new corrugations and his eyes were not just bleary but sad. Her heart went out to her only son. The old familiar urge to love him better briefly, like a distant call, seemed to stir in her but then vanished like a summer breeze in a heat wave. Good old Saint Jude wasn't up to it. Finally the words came. "Adams, this is Mr. Mallory." She spoke slowly as if she were carving each one out of the most unforgiving stone. "He is the landscape architect who has done this wonder." She gestured with her good arm. Her other arm was held by Tristan. Would Adams think that was odd? That she was not using her walker?

"Mr. Mallory is taking me on a tour of the garden. Mr. Mallory." She did not even turn her head to look at Tristan. "This is my son, Adams."

"We'll come around," Tristan said easily.

He shouldn't have said *we*, Maggie thought. He should have said, *I'll bring your mother around.*

168

When they got around, Adams was standing by the new walk.

"Whazz zis?" he said, gesturing with his martini glass at the walk.

He's drunk! Maggie realized and was absolutely furious. "It's a walk, and I've actually learned how to walk on it." Maggie felt her heart racing.

"Must of cost a pretty penny."

"Actually nothing," Tristan said. "I had a lot of leftover stone, couldn't get credit for it. The Steins were perfectly amenable to me using it here. They would have had to pay to dump it."

"Dump it," Adams said dully.

"Yeah, dump it."

"What about labor?" He stared at Tristan with an arrogance that Maggie would never forget.

"No cost," Tristan replied in a leaden tone Maggie had never heard.

"Why, that was very kind of you."

"I don't like to see ladies falling down in their gardens."

"You fell down, Mother?" Adams cocked his head and waited for a response. He looked exceedingly stupid to Maggie.

"Yes, dear. I did. But I am much better now because of this walk and the practice I can do on it."

"Soooo," Adams drew out the word. "You're not only a gardener but a physthic . . ." The word was not coming out right. "A physical therapist."

Maggie thought she would explode. "He's a

169

landscape architect, Adams, and I think you have had too much to drink."

"Oh, you don't say!" There was a definite nasty edge to his words.

Tristan was trying to figure out how to handle this. The guy was a pig! When Maggie talked about her children, reading between the lines Tristan had sensed that she was disappointed in them for reasons beyond the drinking. But he had never expected anything like this.

"Uh, why don't we get your mom up to the house?"

"Good idea. I'll take her from here."

Maggie froze. "Oh, I think I should use my walker. It's just over there."

"Oh, that's not necessary. I can take care of you, Mother."

Before she knew what was happening, he had yanked her good arm and she completely lost her balance. She and Adams were both falling to the ground.

"Jesus Christ!" Tristan roared. "Don't you know what you're doing? You all right, Maggie?"

"I'm fine, I'm fine." She had actually fallen on top of Adams, who was lying on the ground giggling. Then quickly Tristan's words sank in.

"What did you just say to me, old chap?"

Maggie couldn't believe it. Absolute snobbery was the last refuge of pickled Welles minds. Maggie was sitting on the ground facing her son now. She raised her good hand. There was a loud crack.

170

"Mother! You slapped me!"

"You're goddamn right I did. Don't you ever let me hear that tone of voice coming from you again. You are absolutely vile, drunk, a disgrace."

"He can't drive home like this. I'll drive him," Tristan said.

"Call him a cab."

***

"So I guess Adams and I are basically in the same boat," Ceil sighed. "Total failures." She sank down onto the sofa in the living room. Maggie did not like to entertain in the library anymore since it had essentially become her bedroom.

"Total alcoholics," Maggie replied. "We might as well be precise about this. It remains to be seen if you're failures once you get sober. And you're way ahead of Adams. I figured when he showed up here so completely soused he'd come for more than his usual little visit with me. Joan has kicked him out. He's living down at the Tavern Club. They're gentle with drunks. She's already filed for divorce and is going after the house. She's a can-do kind of gal. She'll get it if I know Joan and she deserves it. At least Gordon says if you enter this rehab program and stick with it he won't file for divorce."

"Well, I am entering it. Tomorrow. We leave early in the morning. It's in the Berkshires. Maybe they let you out for Tanglewood for good behavior," she joked weakly.

171

"Look, Gordon is a champ. He loves you. He wants you to succeed. He'd never do like Joan. He knows the kids really love you. Adams has never been much of a father. You are a good mother, Ceil, when you are sober."

Ceil started crying softly to herself. Maggie handed her her handkerchief. Ceil blew her nose, swallowed, then looked up at her mother.

"How come you stuck with Dad?"

"I don't know. Probably the poorest excuse of all: I felt sorry for him."

"Did you love him?"

"I'm not sure," Maggie lied. Once upon a time, before Tristan, she could have said that she was not sure. But now she knew. She just thought it was an awfully sad thing to say to a daughter, that you never loved her father. "There was a genuine affection. And never did your father make a scene like Adams did."

"Adams is worried about money," Ceil said.

"He should be. He doesn't make anything at the brokerage firm. I know he's been going into capital."

"He's worrying that you are."

"Me? Why me? Insurance has covered all the stroke stuff. I just got rid of Mrs. Allen. She and Suzy are the only ones not covered."

"He thinks you're spending more than what is budgeted for the garden."

"That is stupid. I told him Mr. Mallory put in the walk gratis."

"He says that the rest of the garden is looking a

lot better. So he's suspicious."

"Suspicious of what? It's stipulated that I can only take so much from the A Trust for the garden. I don't have any other discretionary funds lying around to do anything with."

"He's convinced that you fired Mrs. Allen so you could use that money on the garden."

Maggie closed her eyes and sighed. Then turned coldly to Ceil. "Ceil, I am not including you in this statement, but it seems to me that Adams's questioning along these lines strongly suggests that he is just waiting for me to die, and not use up any of the B Trust funds that pay my daily expenses and taxes."

"Oh, Mother, how could you ever think that Adams, your own son, would ever want —"

Maggie held up her hand to stop her. "Because, my dear, he is an alcoholic." She paused and the color drained from Ceil's face. "Ceil, I have been the only sober member of this family for two, nearly three generations. I have seen what it does to people. We like to think that only the Kennedys do outrageous things when they are drunk. But let me tell you, although the Welleses are more discreet in terms of public appearances, they have a venality that comes out when they are drunk that can be absolutely appalling. Do you know why your father put that stipulation in his will about the garden budget?"

"No, why?"

"It was because I had signed him into Maybanks, that very expensive drying-out place

173

in Connecticut. The cost of one week at Maybanks was what I spent on the garden in one year. He was so furious that he changed his will just to spite me. I didn't know anything about it. And probably, knowing your father, he would have changed it back. He was always full of remorse. But unfortunately he died of a heart attack in the car as we were driving him to Maybanks, as you well remember."

"Oh, Mom!"

"Ceil, it's too late for your dad. I think it is too late for Adams. But you have a very supportive soul in Gordon. Don't blow it. This Welles thing is a curse, but it does not have to be your destiny."

Ceil had begun to cry softly again. Maggie got up and made her way over to her to give her a pat and a hug. She looked up. "Mom, you're using a cane now."

"Yes." Maggie smiled brightly. "I've graduated from the walker to a cane. Isn't it wonderful?"

"It is," Ceil said softly, looking directly at her mother. "You know, Mom, I think we're all jealous of you."

"Of me? Why, in heaven's name? I'm a sixty-one-year-old wreck."

"But Mom, you're the only one in the entire family who has accomplished a goddamn thing. Look, a year ago you nearly died. You were left half paralyzed, could hardly speak."

"Well, one shouldn't have to have a stroke to prove oneself."

"It's not just that, Mom. Look at your academic record at Regis. Summa cum laude." All Maggie was thinking of at the time was that it didn't amount to a hill of beans if you couldn't raise two productive children and hadn't had the brains to get out of a stupid marriage, not to mention getting into it in the first place. "You even look good, Mom." Maggie made a face. "So who cares if your hair's more gray than red, and you've got a few wrinkles." Instinctively Maggie put her hand to her mouth. "You've got a very good figure for your age. Better than me."

"When you stop drinking and start eating right you'll get rid of that pot." There was a classic alcoholic female figure among Welles women. Adams's sisters Nina and Lannie both had it. They looked liked Humpty-Dumpties — skinny little twig legs and no bottoms, but a barreling out of the whole torso from the pelvis to the chest.

"So Mom," Ceil said as they stood in the doorway, "this is it for six weeks. Wish me luck."

"Oh I do, darling. You have a lot more to live for than a drink. I just know it."

"You can come visit me, you know."

She knew but she really didn't want to. "Yes, I know. And I'll be sure and write." She kissed Ceil, gave her a hug, and stood in the door waving good-bye as Ceil went down the walk to her car. Then she shut the front door and leaned heavily against it.

Maggie had been absolutely exhausted by her

children in the past two days. First the scene with Adams, triggered by the fact that his wife was finally throwing in the towel and was definitely going to want a lot of money in a divorce. And then Ceil. Ceil at least for the moment seemed to be making all the right moves. And Adams, to the contrary, was making all the wrong ones — checking into the Tavern Club rather than rehab, succumbing to paranoia about how she, Maggie, was using money, and now she wouldn't be surprised if Adams began flirting with some of those stupid venture capitalist fellows. He had already lost a bundle through one scheme. It was really not a surprise to her then that Adams was worried about money. It was a surprise that he was suspicious about her use of the funds from the A and B Trusts. The B Trust was her money. She was appalled by Adams's sense of entitlement in reference to this fund. There wasn't that much, but even if she were feeling flush and wanted to spend some on the garden, she couldn't. She wasn't sure what upset her more — Adams's suspicion or his sense of entitlement.

The entire episode with Adams had been shocking. Tristan, however, had been wonderful in the way he had handled it. Perhaps the best part was that Maggie had felt no need to apologize for her son's behavior. There seemed to be a tacit understanding that to do so would be ridiculous. Although Maggie and Tristan had known each other for little over a month he seemed to understand her, where she came from on a moral, spiritual, and intellectual level, and most importantly, he understood that she was indeed an alien within her own family.

She liked it immensely that he often called her Flaherty. "Hey Flaherty, haul that cute butt of yours over here and help me tie back this vine!"

"Hah!"

"What are you hah-ing about?"

"My cute butt, what else! Thank God you didn't say it's perky. I hate perky."

He called her Flaherty the first time he had proposed the cane instead of the walker. "Flaherty, don't give me a lot of trouble about this, but I've hidden your walker. It's time for you to start with the cane." And that was how she had begun walking with the cane. Tristan was there to coach her, of course. He had gone to the library and checked out a physical therapy book and read the chapter on making the transition from walker to cane. It was one of those three-pronged affairs. "By the time we go to New Hampshire you should be proficient with a cane."

"New Hampshire?" This took Maggie entirely by surprise. She knew about his place in New Hampshire. The sea-walled garden, the meadow, the woodland garden that went down to a bog where there were rafts of lady's slippers, but she never imagined him taking her there.

"Yes, New Hampshire. We've got to go there end of the summer, that's when the meadow will be the best." Every year, Tristan told her, he actually planted an entire meadow with annuals and field flowers. Each year it was different. One year it had been all sunflowers, over one hundred different species. Another year it had been shifts of colors from palest pinks to the most intense reds. Various artists and art classes came to paint the meadow.

"Come on, you got almost three months to work on walking. You got to start with the cane. You need a cane to get to the dining room in the vegetable garden. The walker won't fit."

"The dining room in the vegetable garden! What in heaven's name is that?"

"I made it for my girls. It started out as a clubhouse. You know how all kids want a clubhouse. I had already made them a tree house, but Ruthie came up with this idea that she wanted a room in the very center of the vegetable garden with walls that 'are just like real walls, Daddy, and a place for furniture.' So we planted a square of sunflower seeds and by August we had grown sunflower walls. Then the girls got the idea that it could be a kind of outdoor hidden dining room. So we put a table out there. They wanted it to look like a real dining room table and not just a picnic table. So I actually built a round one out of teak. We planted marigolds around the inside perimeter of the room. Not my favorite flower but they keep the bugs away. From the edge of the vegetable garden you never know it's there. You just see this tall stand of sunflowers.

There's no real path to it. You just have to know which row of lettuce to go down. Then you come upon it."

"So you've kept it up all these years."

"Of course. I plant it every year. You'll see it when you come. It can be a bedroom, too." He laughed.

"Did you do other gardens with your girls?"

"A few. They're all still there, too."

"Tell me about them."

"Well, the first one we ever did was the Peter Rabbit garden. It was supposed to be Farmer MacGregor-proof."

"How did you do that?" Maggie asked.

"Oh, the girls painted signs. NO MACGREGORS ALLOWED. RABBITS WELCOMED. We made cold frames just like the illustrations in the book and planted radishes and carrots, all that stuff. Then, I remember, right after my wife and I split up, the girls and I made the Wizard of Oz garden."

"Were they always about books, the gardens?"

"The early ones. Because the girls always just wanted to throw a mess of seeds in the ground. But you know every garden has a story. So I told them to find a story that they loved and we'd work it into a garden. The Oz garden is great. I found some beautiful rocks with yellow lichen for the yellow brick road. They lead to a creek bed and we planted it with watercress. That's Emerald City. So you see, Flaherty, you've got to learn how to use the cane. We've got to go to New Hampshire so you can see all this."

Maggie had not been able to get back to sleep after Tristan had left in the early dawn. She kept thinking of the gardens he had described making for his daughters. She tried to think if she had ever really made anything for Ceil or Adams. She had remembered when they were very young trying to give them each a small plot of land and some seeds, but they weren't in the least bit interested. Maybe she should have tried harder. But had she ever made anything with them? There was a dollhouse that Ceil had been given and she seemed to have a dim recollection of gluing up some odd bits and scraps for furniture. Yes, a clever chair made from a spool of thread and a wood shaving, but oh, for heaven's sake, that had been her mother. No, it was Monsignor John who had made the furniture. It all came back to her now. Adams Sr. had had to check into a hospital. A cancer scare. They ran his liver through the works. Not cancer at all, just alcohol. They were so relieved that Maggie hadn't even cared when he celebrated with drinking an entire bottle of champagne, followed, no doubt, by several vodka chasers. Her mother had come to stay with the children during that time. She had brought the dollhouse and Monsignor John had been over constantly. She'd been too busy with Adams to pay any attention to the children and new toys.

Wasn't that always the way it was? Maggie supposed she was classic in that sense; fit the profile of the alcoholic's wife to a T. She was the *enabler,* the term used in all the literature about addictions, and enablers of alcoholics told themselves countless times every day that they did not have time for dollhouses and making itty-bitty furniture for their children, or clubhouses, or a room with sunflower walls. All their attention must focus on the spouse. No wonder Ceil retreated to that cold, lonely place and did not know how to furnish it.

Maggie went over to the desk and took out a piece of her stationery. She had tried to write Ceil once in the short time she had been hospitalized. The letter had been not much more than a pep talk. Psychobabble about how she knew Ceil could do this, how she knew Gordon loved Ceil passionately. She knew no such thing. Her writing had all seemed so forced, the phrases so hollow. Maggie wasn't a shrink, why did she try to act like one in her writing? There were very few things that Maggie felt she could do well: she could plan a garden and make things grow; she could not, however, furnish the rooms of Ceil's mind. Still she could try to be honest in a letter. Good grief, she supposed she was indeed becoming one of those Cambridge ladies e. e. cummings wrote about "with their furnished souls." Where to begin?

Dear Ceil,

I took off my shoes today while I walked on the stone path Mr. Mallory made. I could feel the im-

pression of a millions-of-years-old fossil, a cri-noid, an ancient lily, on my bare foot — the right foot; the left still does not have much feeling. It's odd thinking about something maybe twenty million years old touching one's foot. Until the rock was split open by the stone masons, no human eyes had ever seen the fossil print. The sun had not warmed it for millions upon millions of years. And then I suppose that no hands had ever touched it except the stone mason's and Mr. Mallory's. And now my foot is the first human bare foot to touch it. Makes me tingle just to think about it. Even the stupid old left side that never tingles almost does. I have nothing else to write. I love you.

Mom

The day Maggie had written this letter, Tristan had to go up to his office in New Hampshire and was due back the same evening. She had been using the cane constantly all that day. She hoped he would see her improvement. Although she was upset about Ceil, she thought now about Adams and the terrible episode. When it had happened, beyond the shock, there was something else. She had felt it even before Ceil had told her about Adams's worry over the money and the trusts. Something had begun to turn, some inexorable force, a meanness had crept into her home that had been brought by her own son. She could not put her finger on it exactly, but something definitely had changed in

Adams's brain. She wondered if he felt it himself, the way she had when her mind began to feel queer just before her stroke.

She went to put on her gardening clothes. Tristan had said not to worry about dinner. He would bring something.

He met her in the first step garden. He had brought a chilled bottle of Veuve Cliquot and a huge pot of yellow star jasmine in full bloom.

"Oh my goodness, Tristan dear, where did you ever get that?"

"From my garden in New Hampshire. See that stump over there?" He pointed to a moss-laden stump just outside the step garden. "I think we should put it there. It will trail off it beautifully and that's the prevailing wind direction, so you'll get to have its fragrance all through the step gardens.

Because the step gardens had escaped the worst of the ravages of neglect and the onslaught of invaders such as wall pepper, and even though there was always something to do in them, the gardens seemed to improve visibly within minutes. Now in early June the Madonna lily had unfurled in all her alabaster glory and in the waxing full moon the lily glowed more intensely each night.

The first step garden was where they usually made love because it had the softest moss. But Maggie had begun transplanting some down to the second step garden. Tristan would joke, "How's our bed coming down there, Flaherty?"

Now he poured her a glass of the champagne. "Got any Monsignor John stories for me this evening?" Maggie had finally told Tristan about Monsignor John, the Flaherty's priest in Charlestown and closest family friend for over forty years. Tristan seemed to delight in what he called her Monsignor John stories: there were Monsignor John and the altar guild ladies stories, Monsignor John and the Cardinal Cushing stories (the latter cheated at cards, but thought no one knew it), there was Monsignor John taking confession from Slippy Ricky, a small-time Charlestown thug who got himself mixed up with the Mafia in a bad way. They were waiting for him right outside the church and gunned him down on the corner. Monsignor John had chased the car, his priest robes flying, all the way down to Warren Avenue. Maggie, nine or ten years old at the time herself, had just rounded a corner and did not know what had happened. "I just thought he looked like Superman. His hair was streaming back, his robes and surplice!" She thought a moment now. "Did I ever tell you about the girl who gave birth in the confessional?"

"What? You got to be kidding."

"Nope. It's the truth. And she hadn't come to confess about that at all. As a matter of fact, she was a star pupil, very scholarly. Colleen Wedge. She and I were always competing for awards and stuff in school. The nuns loved her. Nobody knew she was pregnant and what she came to confess was back-talking her mother. Normally I wouldn't have known this, because Monsignor John never told what people said in confession. I think some priests do, even though they are not supposed to. But I was always badgering him for information."

"Maggie!" Tristan was genuinely shocked.

"Well, I did. I was nosey. You have to understand. I was very close with Monsignor John. He was like a surrogate uncle or maybe grandfather for me, although he wasn't that old, and he tolerated just about anything I did. And being an only child I was already fussed over quite a bit. Monsignor John was rather like the frosting on the cake. But I really don't think you can love a child too much. You can spoil a child but not love one too much." She paused and thought of Adams. "Do you know, I once went to confession and confessed to Monsignor John how I felt bad about badgering him to tell me other people's confessions?"

"You did?"

"Yep."

"What did he do?"

"He burst out laughing and told me to get out of the booth — no penance, no Hail Marys, no Our Fathers — because he knew I'd be badgering him again in no time. I was a remorseless sort of kid. So I guess he thought, what's the use. He was very smart. But anyhow, this Colleen, she gets in there. And she begins: 'Bless me, Father, for I have sinned. . .' 'Yes, my child, and what sins have you committed?' " Tristan wrapped his arms around Maggie and buried his head in the space between her shoulder and neck. He loved her slow voice when she told stories, the Irish lilt crept in, a fragile music seemed to swell the air around them. This could be just about heaven, he thought: his tongue tingly with the Veuve Cliquot, the smell of the jasmine, and this mesmerizing voice. He put his head on her shoulder and slid his hand under her shirt. He could feel her heartbeat.

"You're distracting me, dear. But I'll forge on. So Colleen talks about how she was back-talking her mother. Of course everyone talks about that in Charlestown when they have a really big sin. Back-talking parents, especially mothers, is the camouflage sin of preference for Roman Catholics of Charlestown, and here Colleen's been back-talking her mother for months. It must have been getting boring for him.

"Anyhow, he's thinking that maybe Colleen has actually cheated on a test or something, because she was terribly competitive academically. So he makes a mental note to go over to the high school and talk to Sister Agatha when all of a sudden he hears what sounds, well, he described it as a little hiccup. He doesn't think that much about it. People hiccup sometimes in confession. They even fart . . . yes, that I got out of Monsignor John. He had a lot of funny farting-in-mass stories. But he hears this little hiccup and then a kind of gasp. 'Are you all right dear?' he asks.

'Oh, fine Monsignor, just fine.' But then he hears a grunt. 'Colleen?' 'Just fine, Father. Got a little cramp . . .' She waits a few seconds and gasps. 'It's in my leg.' Lying through her teeth in a confessional, can you beat it? Tristan, are you paying attention, darling?"

Tristan took his hand out of her blouse and looked up. " 'Just fine, Father. Got a little cramp . . . in my leg,' " he said, repeating Maggie's words. She smiled.

"Okay, as long as you're listening." She continued. "So all of a sudden, in the very dim light of the confessional, Monsignor John notices something damp coming through on the carpet from the other side. Finally, it dawns on him that indeed this is not about back-talking parents at all and that in a matter of minutes Colleen Wedge is going to be producing her own little back-talker. So he tears out from his side of the confessional and opens the door on her side. There she is crouched in that little box. Now of course from this point on, I was not given first-hand the graphic details. He told my mother, though, and my aunt. And I overheard them telling my other aunts. He could see this round bulge between Colleen's legs stretching against something. Then he realizes that Colleen still has her underpants on. And he says to her, 'I'm not an obstetrician, child, but I do feel that the first step is taking off your underpants.' So he helps her out of them. There wasn't time to go get anybody. So before you know it there's this little wriggling thing. A baby boy. And Monsignor John ripped off his surplice and wrapped it up. It was big news. They wanted to put it in the *Boston Globe* but Monsignor John stopped that."

"How'd he do that?"

"Oh, Monsignor John was very well connected. I told you how he played cards with Cardinal Cushing. He knew everybody including the editor of the *Globe*. But he wasn't one of those Harvard Club–type priests."

"What's a Harvard Club–type priest?"

"Oh, you know, fancy parishes. There was one from Cohasset. Father Bernard. He was always playing squash at the Harvard Club. Whenever Adams and I went for dinner he'd make a point of coming over and being very Catholic with me. It made Adams quite uncomfortable. Me, too, for that matter."

"How are you 'very Catholic' with somebody?"

"Oh, you know, talking about all these obscure feast days. Once when he knew my mother was sick he said something about lighting a candle for her. God! You should have seen all those old crusty Harvard geezers drop their jaws at that one. Came right over to our table where we were having dinner with Aldena and Randall and I think Posey was there, too; Posey's my niece. She was quite young at the time. She just looked at me like . . . well, I could have been one of those bare-breasted tribeswomen out of *National Geographic*. I mean, that's how exotic all that stuff seems to them."

"So Monsignor John kept it out of the papers?"

"Yes indeed. I, of course, thought it was just spectacular that Monsignor John had delivered the baby. I kept asking him, 'How did you know what to do, Monsignor John?' And he'd just say he didn't know. 'Did you pray? Did you tell her to pray?' I asked. 'No,' he said, 'I told her to push.' Can you beat that!"

CHAPTER 11

Ma

The subtle disposition of Saijo-ji's entry path allows something stirring to take place in the imagination. This experience, called ma *in Japanese, modulates one's sense of space and time . . .*

JULIE MOIR MESSERVY,
Contemplative Gardens

By mid-June the roses were making a gallant effort at a comeback. That there was a green stem left amazed Maggie, but she had fed them with generous amounts of Rosecare along with some other elixir that Tristan had concocted, and soon enough their white blossoms had begun a scramble against the walls and over the arbor. The peonies were as outrageous as they had ever been. Shameless show girls. If Las Vegas had a horticultural exhibit they would have starred, prancing about in all their bosomy bouffant splendor. Where the sunlight became dappled and the garden wilder, stands of iris rose like purple sentries. Near the stone walk, the lupine came back and there was a definite promise of delphinium.

"What did you give them — steroids, dear?" Maggie had asked. She had thought they were gone for good.

"Nothing of the sort. Just cleared out the crap and gave them some breathing room."

Maggie could not help but think that this was a philosophy that had broad applications beyond the realm of delphiniums. Now in the second step garden rafts of ferns had unfurled. Ferns were the one thing that seemed to thrive on neglect and Maggie had never seen them so beautiful. The entire enclosure was a miniature trembling forest of fern fronds. There were at least a dozen different varieties that Maggie had collected over the years. Many had come from Monsignor John's garden at the rectory. He had given her the spores of at least four or five species. The rock from the first step garden that had seemed like a mountain to Tristan appeared majestically through the forest of ferns. In another corner of the garden, a plump mound of veronica quivered with tiny blue blossoms.

Maggie had been setting more of the velvety moss for their bed. She was trying to clear her mind. David Webber had called her to say that he had had a long talk with Adams; that Adams was in very bad shape financially. Was she willing to sell some stock? They could do a transfer from the B Trust to the A Trust and in fact, tax wise it might prove advantageous for Maggie. Maggie had asked for time to think about it. But, in truth, she was tired of thinking about her children and their problems. She had dutifully written Ceil two letters a week so far, but it was hard. She didn't know what to write about. Her life now was the garden and Tristan. She didn't really want to share any of it. She was so content. And as soon as people found out they would begin to ask that ridiculous question: Well, where's it going? At her and Tristan's age, did things have to go anywhere? She had a niggling wonder what would happen when winter came. Maybe she would just go dormant like the old ferns.

It seemed a gross impiety to Maggie to think about winter in the middle of summer. A real perversion of *yugen* and it certainly had nothing to do with tranquility or mystery or the profundity of nature. For some reason, it reminded Maggie of a conversation she had once overheard at a nursery in early spring. A woman was speaking in a very loud voice to the nursery man describing her garden on Beacon Hill. They had just moved into the house a few months before and she had been asked to be on the garden tour. She wanted something that would be guaranteed to bloom the next week. He led her to three squat little azaleas that promised to have a profusion of salmon-colored blossoms open within eight days. This, too, was the opposite of *yugen*. It was better to let a garden go, become old and derelict as she had, than rout everything out, laying down in its place carpets of sod grass, bag loads of fancy mulch, and plopping in a bunch of showy plants guaranteed to bloom on schedule. She could just imagine that woman's garden: all sod grass and that horrid reddish mulch. A blasphemous little affair.

She crawled over to the wood ferns. This was the time to collect their spores. She wanted to harvest some of the spores to start more ferns down in the third step garden. She had also told Tristan that she would give some to the Steins. There was an area that would make a perfect dell for ferns by the waterfall.

The spores of ferns had to be gathered at just the right time. Maggie had had the calendar emblazoned on her brain for years: the time for crested shield ferns was June through September as well as for brake and Christmas ferns. She would give the Steins some Christmas ferns. At least they would not miss that if they were in Nantucket in the summer. This garden that had cost close to a million dollars would be blooming to no audience. Rather like the sound of one hand clapping in the woods, she imagined.

She looked around and tried to spy other ferns with spores that could be collected now. The litany continued in her brain like a soft chant. *Osmunda claytonia,* April through June; oak fern, May and July; woodsia, July and August; chain fern, May through September. She remembered once going down to the Cape with Monsignor John and her mother to collect woodsia that grew near the edge of a cranberry bog. Some of these woodsia might be the offspring from those.

Monsignor John had given her so much for the garden. Every birthday of hers and for each birth of a child and for anniversaries, he would appear with something for her garden. A plant, a cutting. The stone bench had been his gift for her thirtieth birthday. He would often call Adams and suggest things. "You know what I think Maggie Rose would love this year for her birthday? A *Magnolia stellata*. They have a simply lovely one coming up at the Arnold Arboretum auction. Want me to put in a bid?"

"For heaven's sake!" she whispered to herself as she spotted a tiny white cascade of blossoms erupting from a cleft between the rocks of the walls. It was wall pennywort, *Erinus alpinus,* and it had poked through from the third garden below. "Well, bravo for it!" she said.

"Hey Flaherty, talking to yourself again? You're really getting to be a dotty old lady."

Tristan bent down and kissed her. "I didn't even hear you come, dear," she said.

"What are you bravoing about?"

"That!" she pointed to the pennywort. "I planted it down below. It must have climbed up and through. What perseverance."

"Trying to make a show against the saxifrage on the other wall." Tristan nodded to where clouds of pink blossoms were floating behind the thick masses of ferns.

"Yes, aren't they lovely? I used to have some mossy saxifrages but I didn't like them as much.

They're too stiff. I've been collecting fern spores."

"You know you've got a big hole in the wall over there where the rocks fell out. I was going to put them back for you, but it would make a perfect little fern cave. You might take some of those woodsias from the other side. They're so thick you could spare a few."

"I was just thinking about those woodsias. Monsignor John and I went to collect some, gosh, it must have been over forty years ago from the Cape and now it is just dawning on me that these are from the original batch we got. I can so remember him now, coming over with a whole mess of stuff after Adams was born." She sighed. "Guess I'm better with ferns than kids."

Tristan brushed her cheek lightly with his thumb. "Don't do that to yourself, Maggie."

"You're right. Reach me my cane and let's plant the little cave. It will look lovely."

The cave was no more than a foot and a half high by a foot wide, but the small dainty woodsias suddenly created a magical little space. Maggie and Tristan wedged in a mixture of compost and spaghum moss, their fingers glancing off each other's in the dirt. It began to look like a little green cathedral. They were so focused on the space, the rest of the world seemed to fall away. The shadows of ferns played across their faces as they crouched in the dim green light of the second step garden.

Laudaumus te,
Benedicimus te,
Adoramus te,
Glorificamus te.

The words of the Mass came back to her. She could remember so clearly crouching beside her mother and Monsignor John, either in the rectory garden or some woodland where she and he and her mother had gone to collect plants and wildflowers. It was odd. He never had much to do with the altar guild ladies and their strategies for cut flowers throughout the liturgical year; nor had her mother, for that matter. Gardens were their thing.

Suddenly a thought, a thought that perhaps had been lodged in some deep recess of her brain swam to the surface. She turned to Tristan. "You know, I am just now realizing something that I think I have known for years."

"What's that?"

"You won't believe this, but I am sure, absolutely sure it's true."

"What?"

"I am thinking that my mother had an affair with Monsignor John."

"Really? Why?"

"I don't know. The idea just popped into my head." She leaned back. "Tristan, maybe I'm the illegitimate daughter of Monsignor John. It would explain so much."

"Maggie, why would you ever think that?"

"I'm not sure. I mean, my mother really didn't have much in common with my father at all. And now we know how much Catholic priests actually do do it. I mean for God's sake, Tristan, every time you open the paper that's all you read about — their secret sex lives."

"You think he took advantage of your mother?"

"No! No! Not at all. I would like to think that they had a grand love affair like us." Tristan's eyebrows shot up in amusement, his blue eyes flickered. "You don't think that's why I got the Saint Anthony's scholarship, do you?"

"What do you mean?"

"That Monsignor John pulled strings, you know, so his poor illegitimate daughter could be educated. I mean, I like to think that I got it on my own merits."

"You definitely got it on your own merits. I wouldn't worry about that."

Maggie had drawn up her good leg as she sat on the ground so she was resting her elbow on it with her chin cupped in her hand. Tristan thought she looked lovely. Her eyes had that far-away look they sometimes got when she was thinking back to her childhood, to memories of visiting her Nan in Ireland, to the cottage garden where she worked beside her. "Did I ever tell you about the time my tongue froze to the streetlamp?"

"What!" Tristan gasped.

"Yes, it was down on Warren Street in Charles-

200

town. There was a bar there that my Uncle Seamus always went to, you know, Seamus the raging drunk. Well, anyway, I was with my cousin Siobahn, Seamus's daughter. I was about seven. She was a couple of years older than me and her mother, Aunt Sheila, was pregnant. God, it must have been with their sixth or seventh kid. Anyway she had gone into labor and she sent me and Siobahn to get Seamus.

"It was a bitter cold February day. I waited outside because you weren't really supposed to go in. But Siobhan went in and it seemed to take forever. You know how little kids do when they are bored and having to wait someplace. You kind of play with whatever is at hand. I was swinging around the lamppost, dragging one foot, trying to make perfect circles in the snow. I was just flopping about and, don't ask me why, I decided to lick it. Well, my tongue stuck. It was the most awful feeling. I felt it would come right out of my head if I pulled. I just stood there, literally frozen. I kept remembering my Nan telling me a story about how one of her chickens froze to a fence. They finally got him off but one of his legs fell off a few days later.

"I was so stuck and so afraid I could not even turn my head. I could only look in the direction of the Bunker Hill monument. Imagine the Bunker Hill monument as your only view! Well, Uncle Seamus came out. He was drunk, of course, and he says, 'Oh, Mother! What's this wee little girl doing a kissing the lamppost?' I gargled something and Siobhan quickly got the picture. 'She's stuck, Dad. She's gone done stuck herself to the lamppost.' 'Well, that's easily fixed.' He had the smell of drink on him. Uncle Seamus. He moved in a cloud of Guinness. He was his own weather front, so to speak. Anyhow, I could feel his hands starting to pick me up. And just at that very instant, Monsignor John arrives.

" 'Holy Mother of God! You're going to rip out her whole blessed tongue,' he screams and throws himself at Seamus. 'Siobhan! Go in and get a shot of whiskey.' Paddy himself came tottering out with this tiny glass of whiskey. Monsignor John meanwhile had been whispering in my ear the whole time. 'Now don't you worry, Maggie Rose. This isn't going to hurt. It'll be all right, darling.'

"He sort of cradled my head and then he told me to tip my head back very slightly. And he stuck his finger in the shot glass and dabbed some of the whiskey on my tongue just where it met the lamppost. It was like a weird little communion.

"I felt Monsignor John's fingers on my tongue and the hot sting of the whiskey and his soft voice. He could have been saying the Agnus Dei. *Agnus dei, qui tollis, peccata mundi, miserere nobis* — oh, what a doggone shame it was when they got rid of the Latin. Anyhow, Monsignor John peeled me off that lamppost as gently as can be. He lifted me in his arms and carried me all the way home. Right up Soley Street to our own house on the corner of Soley and Wallace. He carried me up the stairs, all four flights. He set me down in the kitchen and he said to Mum, 'Well, ye can thank me for giving the child her first taste of whiskey, Maureen.'

" 'What are you talking about, John?' my mother asked. She said 'John.' I remember at the time I thought it was funny. Mother never just called him John like that. It was always Monsignor John.

" 'You want to tell her, Maggie Rose?' She turned to me, and you know now I do remember there was this frightened look in my mother's eyes and it had nothing to do with the whiskey. No, there was an intimacy in his voice, a kind of pride, now that I think of it, that is reserved for parents and not priests or children. I can remember my mother fretting madly with her apron. Worrying the hem of it in her hands, the way she always did when something bad or frightening was happening. 'You tell her, Monsignor,' I said. I wasn't sure, I suppose, if my tongue was up to it. I kept sticking it out and stroking it because it hadn't felt quite real for so long. There had been the numbness at first, and then the terrible fear of its tearing and then this hot burning liquid — the very fumes made my eyes water. My first drink! No wonder I've never taken to it in a big way."

She sighed, and pressed her lips together. Tears brimmed in her eyes. "So I do believe that dear man was my father." She turned to Tristan. "I hope he knows that I know now."

Tristan took Maggie in his arms. She buried her head in his neck. "Maggie, Maggie," he said softly.

She pulled away a bit. "You know I never told anyone that story."

"Maggie — " Tristan said.

"Oh dear." She was suddenly embarrassed. "I have been rattling on."

"No, Maggie, you've been talking. You've been telling me some of the most fascinating things, stories, I have ever heard."

"Well, you know I am Irish, after all." She smiled and the green in her eyes danced.

"Maggie, I love you. I love you more than anything on this earth."

"And I love you, Tristan."

"So what do we do?"

"Do? Do we have to do anything? Except keep on loving each other?"

"Yes, yes . . . but this fall . . ."

"Oh, Tristan, don't talk about fall and winter, not now, not in the middle of summer. Look! Look what I've learned to do all by myself." Maggie lifted her bad arm with her good one and the fingers began to curve and they held the left side of her shirt so that her right hand's fingers could begin unbuttoning the buttons. And then she lifted both her hands — which she had never before done — to her shoulders, and she slipped off her shirt. Her breasts were washed in moon-light. "Now watch this!" she whispered. She took the cane and with no help she staggered to her feet. Then she dropped the cane and opening her trousers let them fall around her feet. "One last trick!" Her eyes were as green as the ferns. She again lifted her bad arm with her good and unloosed her hair. It tumbled down around her shoulders, gray and auburn with a ruffled dewiness like the fronds of a smoke bush.

Tristan took in every inch. She was the most beautiful and magical creature in the garden, on earth!

CHAPTER 12

"Water"

Kare means "dry," san means "mountain," and sui means "water"; thus a karesansui is a "dry mountain water" garden. . . . Built to aid Zen monks in their quest for enlightenment . . . karesansui gardens feature . . . an abstraction of elements that allows the meditator to forget the physical self while pondering the meaning of the universe.

JULIE MOIR MESSERVY,
Contemplative Gardens

Maggie was working in the third of the step gardens. And although it was an unbearably hot day she felt cool in the garden with its suggestions of "water." The garden was the most beautiful she had ever seen it. Planted over fifteen years before, she had used contrasting mosses through which the wind and light played. It indeed did appear at times like a deep green sea and at other times, particularly at night, like a moonlit lake, still, tranquil. The ornamental grasses at the edge suggested rivers feeding into the moss sea.

There was not a drop of water in the garden, yet it seemed to flow, and sometimes brim and spill with water. Many Japanese "dry" gardens used rocks and raked gravel to suggest the elements of water and wind on water. Maggie had used only two varieties of moss and one type of grass. Light and wind entered the garden and changed the appearance of the moss and grass in the same way they transformed the water of a pond or sea, alternately making darker and lighter patches through passing cloud covers or ruffling the surface with a breeze. She had originally shaped the land in the southeast corner to resemble a promontory of sorts, and she had found one dwarf pine that over the years she had pruned to appear ancient and windswept by the "sea" from its vantage point on the promontory. With its contorted branches that spread like gnarled fingers across the river of grass, it was the perfect expression of the concept Japanese gardener priests called *shizen* — or deep nature. At the base of the promontory was the garden's single rock. It projected into the sea of moss and looked like a small peninsula. It was the ideal place to sit and dip one's bare feet into the "water" made by the hair cap moss.

She knew that Adams would be coming soon. He had called this morning and asked if he might drop by for a visit. Of all the step gardens she did not want him to find her in this one. She actually preferred not to meet Adams in the garden at all. She got up with the help of her cane, which she had learned to manipulate quite easily now, and made her way to the flowering beds near the house. Along the path a stand of shoulder-high thalictrum, lavender mist, trembled on their slender graceful stems. They always reminded her of Japanese women with parasols. Now they seemed to nod as she passed by.

The peonies had long gone by, but their foliage was still lovely. She paused to admire it and marveled once again at the lovely way in which peonies went by. Not like some flowers. Certain roses when they died wound up looking like old wet mops, or delphiniums, which left behind denuded spectral stalks. To die well as a flower, Maggie always thought, was a special gift. The death itself of a peony was lovely in a certain way. It was like a silent crash of petals leaving vivid heaps of pink and white on the earth. She moved on and came to an immense cluster of bright eyes phlox, still slightly incredulous that they had actually come back. Last August there had been barely a bloom. But now they were all batting their crimson-centered eyes. The wall pepper had been the thickest here, but once they had torn it out and heavily dosed the phlox with fertilizer, the plants had begun to bud out with a vengeance.

In less than two weeks she would be going with Tristan to New Hampshire. They planned to spend the Labor Day weekend there. He had some early blooming sedums that he was especially anxious for her to see. She had not yet decided how she would tell the children of her visit to New Hampshire. Ceil, of course, was still in the hospital and Adams had only been over a few times since the disastrous day in the garden.

She heard a car drive up and then a door slam. She concentrated very hard on putting the ugly scene out of her mind. She had to do this every time Adams came. She was glad Suzy was there to let him in and lead him out to the garden.

"Hello, Mom . . . why, look at you! On a cane."

"She's been on a cane for three weeks," Suzy said brightly.

"Didn't you notice it before, Adams?" Maggie asked.

"I guess not. Hey, and look at this garden! It's flourishing. Why don't we have drinks out here."

"Well . . . uh . . ." Maggie stammered. The idea of having a drink with Adams in the garden was appalling to Maggie. "I'm awfully warm, dear. Been out here most of the day, pruning and the like. Perhaps we could go inside. Suzy has set things up for drinks in the living room."

"Sure. But maybe I could just have a quick turn here in the garden to see all you've done."

"Fine," Maggie said, although she hated the idea. She prayed that he would not go down to the step gardens. She did not want him in the step gardens!

"I'll go in and see if I can scrounge up a little nibble of an hors d'oeuvre with the drinks."

Ten minutes later they had settled into their customary spots in the living room. "Well, it's really quite remarkable, Mother. The garden is back to its glory. I can't believe you're doing this all by yourself and within budget."

Adams had repeatedly been asking leading questions about the garden. She was sick of it and she decided right then that it was time to tell him about her friendship with Tristan and how he was the one who had helped and often gave her the materials that she needed.

"Adams," she put down her drink. "I am not quite sure what you are driving at with this sudden interest of yours in the garden, but I want to be as truthful as possible with you."

"Yes, Mother?" He leaned forward slightly.

"I have not spent one penny more than what is authorized. I have had the help of someone, someone who has become quite important to me over the last couple of months." She saw Adams suck in the corners of his mouth just the way his father always had when he was dealing with something slightly unpleasant — it could be anything from a rancid smell to a fall in the stock market to the fact they were out of vodka. "Tristan Mallory and I have become quite close."

"Wwwhat?" Adams took a large swallow of his martini.

"Yes. We are quite close."

"Is this serious?"

"I would like to think that any relationship is serious."

"Relationship!" he nearly spat out the word. A

myriad of emotions crossed her son's face. It all took place within a split second — the shadowy traces of awe, puzzlement, and finally jealousy. Ceil had been right: they were jealous. Ceil's words came back to her. *But Mom, you're the only one in the entire family who has accomplished a god-damn thing. Look, a year ago you nearly died. You were left half paralyzed, could hardly speak . . . Look at your academic record at Regis. Summa cum laude.*

And now she had succeeded again where they had failed. She had not only survived a pathetic marriage and acquitted herself with dignity throughout it, she had found a new relationship. Their own lives were falling apart and hers was coming together. But the look on Adams's face was now not just jealousy. It was disgust. He knows we've had sex. He hates it, Maggie thought.

"I can't believe that what you are saying, what I am hearing, is true."

"I don't know why you find this so impossible, Adams. I mean, people do fall in love . . ."

"Fall in love!"

Maggie leaned forward. "Yes, fall in love."

Adams started to speak. He stopped and then started again. "All right, he's a landscape archi-tect." She knew he had started the first time to say gardener. "But we know nothing about him."

"*You* know nothing about him. I know plenty."

"How do you know he's not after your money?"

Maggie felt the agitation in her building. "I find your behavior shameless. I refuse to discuss this any further. I shall only say one thing. He has more money than I have. So maybe he should be thinking I'm after his. And the reason he has more money is that he's made more money than anyone in the last three generations of this family."

"But Mother, we know nothing of him."

"I know that he's not a drunk. I know that I was nobody — an Irish girl from Charlestown and the Welles family never knew anything about me."

"Well, what are you planning on doing with this man?"

Maggie felt a terrible rage clawing inside of her. "Doing? What business is it of yours? For God's sake, Adams, I am sixty-one years old. I can do whatever the hell I please."

There was something very unnerving about the way Adams kept staring at her over the rim of his glass as he drained his martini. He set the glass down with a shaking hand. "I'm sorry that it has had to come to this, Mother."

"Come to what?"

But he got up and walked out of the room without answering her. She heard the front door slam and then within a minute or two his car pull out of the driveway. For the first time in months her left eye felt jumpy. She had become very negligent about wearing her eye patch. She must be more disciplined about that.

She fetched her eye patch and went outside to the garden, the third step garden again. She sat down on the single rock in the garden, slipped off her shoes, and burrowed her feet in the moss. All the ugliness, the rage began to seep out of her as she felt herself drawn into this miniature world with it seas and rivers. A slight wind ruffled the ornamental grasses, turning them into the liquid stream. There was even a visible current as a narrow swath of the grass turned its dark side toward her. The very few splinters of light that penetrated the shady canopy spilled across the moss like flitting minnows. There was a subtle stirring in Maggie's imagination, in her mind's eye, as she watched the light that seemed like fish. The moss trembled when a slight breeze shivered the still water in the middle of the lake. This is what happens here, Maggie thought. This is the place where time nearly stands still and space contracts until the universe is at one's feet. Was she shrinking or was she growing larger? The spirit of the place filled her and yet at the same time, some of her flowed out into the deep nature of the third step garden. Here, she was in balance; here there were no beginnings and no endings. Here, all was one and continuous. Maggie did not have to turn around to feel the presence of the tree that she had nurtured and pruned for years. She felt its ancient spirit enfolding her.

That night, Maggie and Tristan slept the entire night in the garden. It was the first and only time they would ever do this. They brought out light cotton sheets to cover them. They made love three times. Maggie felt the moss under her and between her legs. She felt the soft night wind curling around their bodies. They were whales, they were islands, they were underwater meadows of endless colors within an endless sea. The next morning Tristan had to leave early to fly down to Nantucket for three days and then directly to New York for another day or possibly two.

It was an unusually cool morning for August when Maggie decided to take her first walk with her cane outside of the garden. She actually intended to go out of Lennox Circle and walk the three blocks to Harvard Square. She knew she was up to it now. And she was. When she returned, she found a man and a woman by the gate to her house, peering intently at it. She saw the man take out a camera. "I don't know whether I can get it all in the frame, Helen. This is really not a wide angle."

"Why don't you go across the street and then take it at an angle, you know, the northeast-southwest axis."

Maggie got the queerest feeling in her stomach. She walked up to them.

"May I help you?" she asked.

"Oh, just taking pictures of the house for the office."

"What? What office?"

"Bullocks."

"Bullocks!" Bullocks was a Boston real-estate firm. She had heard of it, but no one in Cambridge dealt with Bullocks. It was definitely not upscale.

"Well, why are you doing that? I happen to be the owner of this house."

"Oh, oh . . ." the couple seemed temporarily flustered. "Oh, Mrs. . . . ."

"Mrs. Welles."

"Yes, Mrs. Welles, uh, we were told that this might be coming on the market."

"What?" Maggie was speechless. "Who told you that?"

"A . . . a Mr. Donahue."

"I don't know a Mr. Donahue and the house is not for sale."

"There must be some mistake," the woman named Helen said feebly.

"Yes," the man agreed. "Some mistake. Sorry for the inconvenience."

The two hurried off down the sidewalk. But Maggie could tell that they were not sorry and it was not a mistake.

"David Webber, please." Maggie gripped the phone. "What? He's on vacation . . . what? Oh, oh. I see. Well if he does call in please tell him to call Margaret Welles immediately. Uh . . . oh, let

218

me think about that. Yes, I think I have met Mr. Matthews. Yes . . . thank you . . . good-bye."

Maggie set down the phone. David Webber was on a rafting trip down the Colorado River with his family and was absolutely unreachable for ten days. She had to get to the bottom of this. Tristan wouldn't be back for another five days or more. He was supposed to go from Nantucket to Long Island where he was doing a big project in the Hamptons, and then possibly out to New Mexico to meet with a new client. If he was going to New Mexico he might go on for a one-day trip to San Francisco where he was to check up on the final stages of a job for the city. That would add on another three days. God, they would have never been separated this long, but at least when he came back it would be almost time to go to New Hampshire.

Another day or two passed. Tristan had called to say that he would have to go to New Mexico. By this time, Maggie was completely focused on the upcoming trip to New Hampshire and had successfully pushed to the back of her mind the peculiar incident with the people from Bullocks real estate. An old friend had come out and taken her for lunch in the square. When Maggie came back, Suzy said a Dr. Messner, a Lucille Messner, had called and would like her to return her call.

"Did she say what it was about?"

"No, Mrs. Welles, but then again I didn't ask."

"Messner . . . Messner." Maggie turned the name over in her mind. "Suzy, I've had a lot of doctors in the past year, but I don't recall one with the name Messner."

"Me neither."

"Well, I'll give Dr. Messner a call back."

She wasn't in but Maggie left a message that she had returned Dr. Messner's call. Finally that evening around six, Dr. Messner called.

"Yes, Mrs. Welles, Dr. Messner here."

"Yes, Dr. Messner, now what is it I can do for you?" There was a long pause on the other end of the phone. "Dr. Messner?"

"Yes, yes I'm here." Another pause. "Uh, Mrs. Welles, I have been appointed by the court to come and make a visit."

"What?" Maggie was utterly confused.

"Mrs. Welles, you know nothing about this, I gather?"

"Nothing. What kind of doctor are you, if I may ask?"

"I'm a psychologist."

"A psychologist? Are you from the Spaulding Center at Mass General?"

"No . . . no . . ."

"There was a psychologist from Spaulding who saw me briefly after my stroke. A Dr. Golden . . . wha . . . what is this about a court? A court appointed you? I don't understand." Maggie felt something sickening welling up in the back of her throat.

"Mrs. Welles, I am truly sorry to have to tell you this in this way . . ." Her first thought was that something had happened to Tristan. Her eyes widened in horror. "There has been a document filed in probate court requesting a guardian ad litem." Maggie wasn't quite hearing all the words. She just knew that this was not about Tristan. Tristan was okay. Unbelievable relief swept through her.

"Did you hear what I said, Mrs. Welles?" The woman was asking her something.

"Uh, something about a document and probate court."

"Yes. Do you know what a guardian ad litem is?"

Maggie felt like saying that if it wasn't in the Mass, or High Mass, chances were that she did not know the Latin. But she sensed that this was not a time for jokes. There was something so deadly serious in the woman's voice. "No. What is a guardian ad litem?"

"It is someone appointed to take care of your affairs. It can be your business affairs or issues concerning your health care. It is basically a manager."

"And who might this manager . . . this guardian ad litem be?" Maggie asked.

"Your son, Adams Welles."

"Adams . . . !" Maggie gasped. "Adams! My God! He can't even take care of himself."

"Well, apparently there is some question about this entire request. The judge in probate is holding this up pending an evaluation. I have been asked to evaluate you."

"Evaluate me for what?"

"Mrs. Welles, I don't think this is the time to go into all of this right now."

"I do! It's my life. It's my body, my mind, my money that is going to be managed. I think this is a damn good time to go into it, Dr. Messner."

There was another long silence on the end of the telephone. "So your son never said anything to you about this?"

"Absolutely not."

"Nor your lawyer, Mr. Donahue?"

"Donahue?" Maggie repeated. "Donahue? Who's Donahue? Never heard of him. David Webber is our family lawyer and has been for thirty-five years. Donahue!" Maggie nearly shrieked. That was the name of the man the realtors said told them the house might be coming up for sale.

"I think, Mrs. Welles, that I am going back to probate court and, based on this brief conversation with you, inform the judge that all proceedings should halt temporarily."

"Temporarily? Forever! Dr. Messner, I am perfectly capable of handling my own affairs. It is true that I had a stroke a year ago. But since then I have not only learned how to talk again, as I think I should have proven in the last five minutes, but also walk, feed, and dress myself. I keep a very well-balanced checkbook and, I would also like to add that, unlike my two children, I am not an alcoholic. Now I am quite tired, but I intend to get to the bottom of this. Good night, Dr. Messner."

"Good night, Mrs. Welles. I am sorry for disturbing you."

"Well, you certainly did that."

Maggie was shaking so hard by the time she put down the phone she could barely breathe. Her eye had gone wacko again. She went to the library where she still slept and fumbled in a desk drawer for her eye patch. She wanted to think. Her first instincts had been to call up Adams and completely chew him out. But she felt that was not perhaps the best thing to do. She was going to have to be very cagey. She could not believe that Adams had sunk as low as this. She had better call David Webber's office first thing in the morning and get in touch with that associate. Good Lord, she couldn't even remember his name right now. Oh, and she did wish Tristan would call, but he wouldn't be at a place where he could be reached for two days. She would call anyway and leave a message for him. Maybe he would get there early.

She had a positively rotten night's sleep and was so utterly tired it was all she could do to drag herself out of bed and into the shower. She heard Suzy rattling about in the kitchen. She was almost tempted to ask Suzy to bathe her, but it had been so long since she had had to have help. Tristan didn't count when he bathed her. Besides, it wasn't really bathing. It was sex. She laughed at the thought.

After her shower she stepped out onto the patio. "Good God, it's freezing." Within scarcely eight hours the weather had become chilly and there was an autumnal feel in the air. The sky seemed too dark. Maybe it was just her left eye. It was not seeing that well. She must put on her eye patch again.

"Look at that branch over there, Mrs. Welles." Suzy pointed to a maple on the west side of the terrace. Maggie's breath caught in her throat. Amidst the inky greens, one branch, just one, had a limb of bright yellow leaves. She had seen this happen before, in the middle of summer; when you think it will go on forever, one tree decides to have its own private little autumn. It reminded Maggie of the time when she was quite small and it had suddenly begun to snow heavily. Her mother had gone out just a few hours before and had not taken her hat. When she came back her hair was covered with snow.

"I'm a frost creature, aren't I, Maggie Rose?" she had said, and had laughed when she saw herself in the mirror. But Maggie didn't think it was funny. She was not a frost creature. In the space of one morning, her mother had turned gray. She had become an old lady like Nan. Maggie had spent inordinate amounts of time worrying about her Nan in Ireland and what would happen when her Nan died. This was the worst thing that Maggie could imagine. Death, which had never seemed quite real, suddenly was. She knew in that moment when she saw her mother that someday Nan would die and her mother, too. Death was no longer an abstraction.

But now she could imagine another even more terrible thing. Winter. It was coming. In the chill late-August air she felt its course set, inexorable, unflinching, resolute. She could not, in fact, stay a summer against a winter.

CHAPTER 13

Mu

One must forget oneself. It is like trying to see nature's reflection on the surface of a pond rippled by the wind; until the ripples subside, there is no clear reflection. In Zen Buddhism, to reach this point of no-self is called mu. . . .

PROFESSOR KINSAKU NAKANE,
contemporary Japanese garden master,
as quoted by his student Julie Moir
Messervy in *Contemplative Gardens*

"Well, what I see here, Tristan . . ." They were standing on the patio of the woman's newly built house with its spectacular view of the Sangre de Cristo Mountains, "is essentially a kind of desert Sissinghurst. A white garden."

Tristan Mallory swallowed so his mouth wouldn't fall open. A white garden in this land of pinyon trees and endless sky with its subtle spectrum of pinks and blues and lavenders, and mountains that turned blood red in the setting sun? A white garden! The lady was out of her fucking mind! No dusty silvers and greens spiked with turquoise and then a swath of poppies with their chiffon petals to shiver in the desert breezes, or maybe a small walled garden, a tea garden carpeted with sedums and succulents and set with desert rocks, or a bleached antelope skull just out of a Georgia O'Keeffe painting?

Now she was talking about arbors with clematis.

"Uh, I don't think clematis would do well in this soil." How the hell was he going to get out of this one? It was a good job. Lots of money. But he was not the person for this job. He would recommend Garland Washburn. Garland Washburn was to landscaping what Robert Stern was to architecture and Ralph Lauren was to fashion. They were maestros of calling up references to the past; of actually reinventing the past for popular consumption, more perfect than the past had ever been. Doing a white garden for the Steins in New England was one thing, but Vita Sackville-West in chaps on the desert was something else!

Tristan had felt gloomy all morning. He missed Maggie desperately and although he had talked to her two days before and she seemed fine, he had felt anxious for some reason that morning as he had driven out from where he was staying in Albuquerque to Santa Fe. He had the sense that he had experienced some kind of disturbing dream that he could not remember. His anxiety had been increasing throughout the morning. There was a cool westerly wind. Maybe it was that. Maybe it made him think of winter. He just suddenly knew he had to get back east. He and Maggie would go to New Hampshire early. He would try and call her from the airport to let her know that he was skipping San Francisco. They had to go right away to New Hampshire and plan — for what? he thought. Maybe for winter and the rest of their lives.

He tried to call her from the airport but there was no answer. His flight was delayed because weather had become suddenly unsettled in the east, with a chain of tropical storms swirling toward Hatteras. They were talking about rerouting him through Minneapolis.

Maggie peered from behind the curtains of the living room. She had heard a car pull into the circular drive. She had been expecting this. She knew that Adams would not give her any warning. But it was not Adams's car and she had not expected him this soon. When she had finally gotten in touch with David Webber's associate, George Matthews, although he sounded no older than a college student, he seemed extremely competent. He did not seem shocked but genuinely concerned. He knew she was a longtime client of David's. He said yes, what she was telling him was quite alarming and asked permission to have his legal assistant listen in and take notes. He was involved in a big court case and would not be able to come over until the next day. But he was sending an assistant over to probate court immediately. The A Trust did own the house but there was absolutely no way that Adams could sell it without suing the estate.

"What about this ad litem thing?" Maggie asked.

"We're going to quash that in exactly three hours max, Mrs. Welles." George Matthews spoke emphatically. "Don't you worry." He got the names of all of her doctors and said that if necessary he would be taking affidavits from them. He then warned her that under no circumstances should she sign any papers that Adams might present her with.

Adams got out of the car with a man she had never seen. Suzy let them in and brought them into the living room. Suzy looked quite tense. Maggie had told her some of what was happening but she had also told her that she had expected a visit from Adams and no one else. She had never dreamed he would have the gall to bring this lawyer into her own home.

"Mother, this is Mack Donahue. He's actually from Charlestown, Mom."

"Linden Street, near where you grew up, I understand. Went to Church of the Redeemer." He held out his hand. Maggie did not extend hers.

"Are you going to invite us to sit down, Mother?" Adams said.

"Why?"

"Mother!" he said tightly. "Don't make this any more difficult than it has to be."

"I am going to make this more difficult than

you ever imagined," Maggie replied coldly.

Adams turned to Suzy. "Suzy, I think if you would excuse us now."

"No, Adams, she will not be excused by you. She is staying right here . . ." Maggie could feel the tumbrels of her mind turning slowly. "I have already talked to my lawyer."

"David? I thought he was out of town."

"He is. I am sure that accounts for your timing. But there are other lawyers at Hinckley and Bodkin, you know. George Matthews, David's associate, is more than competent and he has advised me that when you came there should always be a witness in the room and Suzy has agreed to be just that. She will be taking notes on this conversation."

George Matthews had advised that Maggie have someone with her, if at all possible, when Adams dropped by. He had said nothing about taking notes. This was Maggie's idea — a spontaneous one at that, or she would have warned Suzy. But Suzy was quick and immediately walked over to the desk and slid open a drawer. She found a small pad of paper. Maggie marveled. The girl was a wonder. Suzy sat down with great aplomb, crossed her legs, and quietly looked at the two men. Adams and Mack Donahue were clearly caught off guard.

"Well, Mother, we just have some very boilerplate forms that we . . ." Donahue shot Adams a venomous glance.

"I think, Adams, we should just talk now," said

Donahue. "I know, Mrs. Welles, that this might have come as a shock to you. You have to understand that this is not irregular at all. This is simply good sensible estate planning . . ." he continued to talk. Maggie did not say a word. Every once in a while they would ask her something and she would simply not speak. Her silence began to unnerve them. They became increasingly bold in their suggestions about her competencies and more vivid in portraying possible end scenarios. Finally Donahue brought out his last straw. "And, Mrs. Welles, about the garden. It is clearly evident that you have exceeded the budget and your relationship with this er . . . uh . . . ."

He's stalling, Maggie thought. He wants me to fill in the name. They are trying to provoke me. But I will not mention Tristan's name here any more than I would take these two foul creatures, these profane men, into my garden. That was where Maggie had begun to retreat as the men spoke on. She had simply in her mind gone to her step gardens. She was on the dewy path. She had just passed the stone lantern and was under the dogwood. In her mind it was still May and the blossoms were out. She entered the first garden — garden of rapture, plush with moss, and from the notch in the wall she could see the rock looming as large as a mountain in the garden below. And then on to the second garden steeped in ferns. She felt her hands in the little cave in the wall where she and Tristan had

234

planted the woodsia. This garden with the susurrahs of the swaying ferns, the deepest shade in the heat of the summer, the scent now of the yellow star jasmine blowing through it was a realm of pure enchantment; it was the place where Maggie had staggered to her feet on her own with only the cane for help, where she had for the first time used her bad arm to undress herself and loosen her hair and then she had stood before Tristan naked and feeling beautiful.

"Mother, have you heard a word we have said?"

"Every single one. And Suzy has them all written down. And now if you'll excuse me, I think it is time for both of you to go. If you want any further communication with me on these subjects you will not get it. You must go to our family's lawyers. And by the way, today they have just initiated action to stop this ridiculous thing you're filing in probate court."

Adams started forward in his chair, anger flaring from his bleary eyes. Donahue put a hand on his arm. "We should go now, Adams. I'm sure everything will work out." He smiled tightly at Maggie.

The men got up to leave. Suzy showed them out. "Oh my God, Suzy, I almost need a drink." Maggie sighed. "But no, get my eye patch, will you, please? It's in the library." She pressed her hand against her left eye. There was a wild pulse beating in it and things kept jumping in and out of focus.

"Mrs. Welles, you were wonderful. And . . . and . . ." Suzy wasn't sure how to phrase what she desperately wanted to say.

"Out with it, Suzy. Frame it, as the speech therapist used to say to me."

"Mrs. Welles, I think all along I have known about you and Mr. Mallory."

Maggie opened her eyes wide. "You did?"

"Yes. I think I knew even before he put in the stone walk for you."

"Really? How?"

"Once early in the spring a stray cat came into the front yard and I thought for some reason it might be the Steins'. I went over there and rang the bell but no one was there. So I walked around to the back and I saw him, Mr. Mallory, looking at you through that crack in the wall. It was like he was hypnotized or something. He just had this indescribable look on his face. Kind of half yearning and half — well, half like he was on the edge of a dream, a very old dream."

"A very old dream," Maggie repeated softly. "How do you mean?"

"I'm not sure. You know how some people spend a life just searching for something and don't really know what for exactly, but they know that somewhere out there it is really there, if they can just get to it. Well, that is how it was with him."

"Oh, Suzy, come here you dear child." Suzy walked over and dropped to her knees by Maggie's chair. "Suzy, I think I really love you. Love you so much." She put her arms around Suzy's strong shoulders.

"You want me to stay tonight, Mrs. Welles, since Mr. Mallory is away?"

"Oh, so you know he's away?' Maggie's eyes twinkled.

"Yeah. I can always tell when he's spent the night."

"You can?"

Suzy turned bright red. "Yeah, the sheets are all swirled up." They both burst into giggles.

"You know, he's taking me to New Hampshire in a few days to see his place. He has a sea garden. It must be beautiful. It goes right down to the ocean. I can't wait."

"Are you sure you don't want me to stay tonight?"

"No Suzy, that's not necessary, but tomorrow when you come I want to take you to a special place in the garden. I don't take many people there. Most people who know me don't even know about it. My late husband never even entered it."

"Where is it?"

"Just at the end of the garden. I call them the step gardens because each one steps down into the next. They are quite lovely and when all the rest of the garden went to wrack and ruin, somehow the step gardens were spared."

"I can't wait, Mrs. Welles."

"Come early. They look wonderful just after sunrise."

CHAPTER 14

Shizen

The Japanese, however, understand naturalness to be something quite different. They call it shizen, *meaning deep nature . . . planting an "ancient" tree in a garden gives the space an aged appearance and a sense of paradox between a garden element that is designed and the unintentional, spontaneous quality found in nature. Thus, the best Japanese gardens leave little obvious trace of the designer's ego, only hinting at human involvement through the images of* shizen *that are created in the minds of the beholders.*

JULIE MOIR MESSERVY,
Contemplative Gardens

After Suzy left, Maggie found herself utterly exhausted. She was not really hungry at all but sat down and ate a bit of yogurt with some fruit. The telephone rang. She suddenly remembered that Aldena had said she would call about taking her to The Country Club tomorrow, the last thing in the world Maggie wanted to do. She decided to let the answering machine pick it up.

"Maggie dear! Aldena here. Bet you're out in the garden. So how about lunch tomorrow at The Country Club? It's not the buffet day so there'll be no problem with your handling your plate . . ." Aldena was so tactful. She rattled on for the better part of a minute, then promised to call back in an hour.

Sure enough in exactly an hour the phone rang. Maggie heard it just as she was coming out of the bathroom. She'd dropped her cane, which delayed her, but she certainly wasn't going to rush to get a call from Aldena. What was she going to say to her sister-in-law? "I'll wear a bib, don't worry about me embarrassing you at The Country Club." She didn't make it in time. The answering machine picked up. It wasn't Aldena. It was a male voice.

"Mrs. Welles, this is Mack Donahue. I know that our meeting this afternoon upset you. But really, there is no reason to be upset. I think you just have to understand that we are all on your side, and just after I left your house . . . well . . . I happened to be down in Charlestown, taking an aunt of mine over to Holy Redeemer and ran into Father Stephen. I believe you know him. He was a very close associate, he tells me, of your family's dear friend Monsignor John and he was . . ." Maggie had stood stock still for unending seconds but the moment Monsignor John's name was mentioned she made her way as quickly as she could to the answering machine and yanked its wire from the socket. It was as if a rankness had begun to fill the house. A poisonous gas seemed to seep into every corner, every thread of fabric.

Maggie tried to calm herself but she suddenly felt that she could not be in the house a moment longer. It was warm out but not hot. It would grow cooler as the evening went on, but Maggie knew that she must go to the step gardens to sleep tonight. She was quite certain she would die if she stayed in the house that night. Surely Tristan would be back soon. She would take a blanket with her. But she felt so tired it was all she could do to haul herself into the library and pull the blanket from her bed.

She stepped out on to the terrace. Warm gusts whipped through the night. It was typical hurricane weather. Boston rarely got the storms as full-blown hurricanes but seemed to be lashed by warm humid air and unsettled weather for days on end. She supposed she should have brought a rain poncho, but she was simply too tired to go back and get it. The day had taken more of toll than she had realized. She began down the ramp. Her left leg was not really responding. She was having to drag it the way she did days back when she used the walker. The light of the moon filtered down gray and shadowy through thick clouds. She could smell fish in the air. It was that hurricane smell, slightly fetid and tidal.

"Oh, my God," she gasped as she stumbled and saw the ground coming toward her. It wasn't a hard fall. The grass was soft. But now she had to get up. She could do it. She had done it before. She patted herself and caught her breath. She just had to get to the garden, the third step garden, because the more she thought about it the more she feared that Adams and the awful lawyer were probably coming for her. They were going to whisk her away someplace. Ceil would have never done this! Now focus, Maggie, she told herself. You must get up! You must get up! But somehow it was so strange — she seemed to have lost track of her leg, her left leg. She couldn't remember where it was. She knew it was on one side of her body, but she actually had to feel with her good arm alongside her rib cage, patting herself down until she came to her hip. It seemed that the leg should be closer and that she was patting forever and could not find it. She was rather astonished about how far away her own leg was. Would she ever get to it? Then she would have to drag it back and pull it under her and get on her knees. She knew the steps, the moves, if she could just find her goddamn leg! She felt clueless and without signals. But finally, there it was! Then it must have taken her another five or ten minutes to get into the position, to raise herself on the cane.

"Come on, you can do it," she whispered to herself. The cane didn't seem to be cooperating as it usually did when she wanted to get up from weeding. It kept slipping out from her hands. "Come on, cane," but the words came out

"Come on, pancake." She finally gave up on the cane and began crawling across the grass. The night when she had first come out had an eerie brightness; however, now it seemed to be growing dimmer. Oddly enough, it was just growing dimmer on one side. Maybe there was some sort of eclipse going on. Would that make one side of the sky dimmer than the other?

She was crawling as best she could. When she got to the peonies she would rest. It seemed like an eternity. The grass was rather soft there and she thought for a moment about taking a little nap under the arbor that was just a few feet away. Take a little nap and dream of the Oz garden Tristan had made for his daughters. And yes, the hidden dining room behind the sunflower walls. But something urged her forward, even though the left side of her body felt stone heavy and her eye was throbbing. It seemed as if she had only a pinprick of clear vision from that eye. A milky halo surrounded everything that was not dead center in front of her. She was beyond the arbor now and not that far from the *roji* path. Why did the air suddenly smell like cinnamon when minutes before it smelled like fish? The wind blew harder and a light drizzle began. She was nearly to the *fumi-ishi* stone, the entry to the dewy path. "Hello stone!" "Hello lantern!" The familiar landmarks appeared along the path. She greeted them but sometimes the word didn't come out quite right. She wondered who that was singing "Happy Birthday." If only Tristan would come. She pictured him rappeling down a limestone cliff against a blue sky and reaching into a wind wedge. "Come soon, Tristan," she whispered and a big tear rolled out of her right eye. The left eye was dry. "I'm waiting for you, dishwasher!" Oh dear, why weren't the words coming out right? Not that again. It was so annoying.

She stopped a moment. She was perspiring heavily despite the rain. Ahead was the Japanese maple that overhung the first of the step gardens. She blinked, but with only one eye. She stared at the maple ahead. There was something in the form of the tree, in the very bark and the leaves. A figure. Oh, it must be like reading pictures into clouds. Maggie giggled. The shape of a person melted out of the branches. It looked just like Monsignor John, the way he would raise his arms when making the sign of benediction. Then she remembered the first time that Tristan had made love to her in the first step garden — how the leaf from this very tree had settled on her stomach just beneath her navel; how he had brushed the inside of her legs with it, how they had made love again.

She had to crawl faster. The grade of the path grew steeper but it was at least downhill and not so hard to drag her leg. She passed the garden of ferns, the garden of enchantment. She would have loved to pause there for a moment for the ferns must look spectacular tossing about in this moon-laced windy night, their shadows dancing

246

like crazed banshees. And of course this was the month to harvest the spores of, what was it — maidenhair and crested shield and Hart's tongue, but in her head she was thinking alternately of their Latin names, *Adaintum pedatum . . . Aspidium cristatum . . . Scolopendrium vulgare . . . Onoclea sensibilis . . .* Now instead of the plant names, she began chanting the Lord Have Mercy chant, the *Kyrie eleison,* though Maggie would have sworn that she was speaking of ferns and not chanting in Latin.

> *Kyrie eleison*
> *Christe eleison*
> *Credo in unum Deum*
> *Patrem omnipotentum*
> *factorem coeli et terrae*
> *visibilium omnium et*
> *invisibilium*

She was almost there! Something was dripping darkly from her mouth onto the path. Had she laughed and bitten her tongue again? No matter, it didn't hurt. She couldn't feel anything on that side of her face. Using the last of her strength she dragged herself into the third step garden. The rain had started to come down harder and the wind had built. But here in the third garden everything seemed still. Not a hair of the moss quivered. The liquid world of shivering moss and grass rivers was tranquil. Maggie floated to the very middle of the moss sea. She lay on her side. Ribbons of moonlight fell through the clouds. The rains seemed to have stopped. The clouds racing over the moon cast their shadows on the moss. And just as the still, glassy surface of a lake reflects the clouds and the mountains and the trees around it, so did the moss sea. And as the splinters of sunlight during the day became fish, these clouds were transformed into reflections of mountains and the streaks of moonlight into schools of dolphins. Maggie remembered reading that a gardener priest had once said that "clouds do not arise over mountain peaks; they fall into the bottoms of ponds."

Maggie's mind grew calmer and more peaceful. She was now in this place of complete tranquility where nothing disturbed the surface of the water and she could see everything. There was no difference between the reflections and the object reflected; one was no more real than the other. The light was closing down in her left eye, but it did not matter. The images came back. She could remember it all. She could see another light coming through the woodland. She could hear footsteps. She was losing consciousness. She would not utter a word. She did not want to say *pancake* when she knew the right names.

"Flaherty!"

CHAPTER 15

*R*esonance

Professor Nakane once said, "Saiho-ji's garden has a lot of dreams." He was right. The Moss Temple is a tapestry of dreams. . . . The spirit of yugen *remains with a visitor long after leaving. . . . It resonates in us like the sonorous chanting of the sutra and lingers like the reverberation of the priests' drum and bell.*

JULIE MOIR MESSERVY,
Contemplative Gardens

Jesus, Joseph, and Mary, will you look at those peonies. Big bosomy show girls . . . oh, look over there, dear, look at that darling thing . . . I guess you're right, she's a lot tougher than she looks.

You know, Flaherty, we should try mixing in some lavender over there, and then maybe where that first retaining wall is on this side of the step garden some more. Lavender against stone . . .

Nothing oooh la la, of course,

Of course dear, of course Flaherty.

You should never have to be beautiful to be in a garden . . . "But you were, Maggie." This time Tristan spoke the words aloud. "And you were rare, too," he whispered as he walked toward the rose-encrusted arbor. He took his Felco shears from his pocket and clipped back a dead-looking branch from a dwarf enkianthus. He peered at the cut. "Wick," he said.

He looked across the lawn to where Ceil stood, her somewhat stumpy figure more slender now that she was back from rehab. She was dry. She seemed stronger. But though she shared Maggie's coloring there was very little that reminded him of Maggie. At best she was a blurred, almost out-of-focus version of her mother. He watched as Gordon came up to Ceil and put his arm around her. It made Tristan feel good.

Ceil stood barefoot on the sun-warmed stone and traced with her toe the impression of the ancient lily. Was hers the second bare foot to touch the twenty-million-year-old fossil? She should stop her daydreaming. The musicians would be coming soon and the caterers might need something.

"So Mr. Mallory, where are these river stones supposed to go?" A voice called out. She looked across the garden at Tristan, who was coming her way. He looked elegant in his cream-colored linen jacket. No black. No maudlin Wasp funeral for her mother. No, this would be as good as any Irish wake. No gladiolas, please. She could see that one of Tristan's pockets was heavy. The Felco shears, she laughed to herself. A landscaped Irish wake! She began walking toward him.

"Right over there, Tony, by each one of those jasmine standards." Tristan raised his arms and inscribed an arc in the air. "Just lay them out around the base so it looks like a pool of water. Make sure that no grass shows through. We're going for a water look here. Right before the people come we'll wet them down."

"Oh Tristan, where did you get those little jasmine trees?" Ceil walked up and lightly placed her hand on his shoulder.

"Cuttings from the one down in the step gardens. Grew them over the winter and grafted them onto some stock I already had. They would have never gotten that tall on their own. Caterers here yet?"

"Oh yeah. They got here forty-five minutes ago."

"Where's Suzy?"

"Helping the caterers."

"She okay, Ceil?"

"Now don't you worry about Suzy. She's going to be just fine. We've had a long talk. I took her out for dinner last night. I got her all excited about going back to school."

Tristan put his arm around Ceil and gave her a squeeze. "Your mom would be proud, kid."

"The question is, how are you doing, Tristan?"

"I'm okay. I'm okay."

"Oh, here come the musicians. Now where did you want them to set up, Tristan?"

"Under the trellis."

"Oh my God, and here comes Adams."

"He came?" Tristan looked across the lawn. Adams looked about the same but he moved with the gait of an old man. "Good," said Tristan.

"It is good, isn't it?" Ceil looked at him, her eyes brimming with tears. "I'm going over to him."

"I'll be over in a couple of minutes." He watched as Ceil, with a quickness in her stride, went up to Adams. She reached up and pulled his face down for a kiss and then took his arm in hers. Maggie would have been so proud of her, he thought, so very proud. Tristan saw their heads huddling together as they traversed the garden slowly.

After Maggie had died Adams had indeed made an attempt to sell the house. But he had neglected to anticipate his sister's response. Sober and with the support of her husband, Gordon, Ceil would not hear of selling the house. She bought out Adams's share. She and Gordon had started over again in the stucco house on Lennox Circle. She had found in her mother's papers some plans for extending the gardens, bringing them actually closer to the house with a kitchen garden, a classic potager. She had shown them to Tristan and he was to begin work early in the spring with the idea of completing them by the time of the memorial service. He had, just in time, the two days before. He had found some dusty old ochre bricks that picked up on the cognac color of the house. He laid them in a slightly eccentric zigzag pattern. Maggie had indicated arrangements of clay pots and large glazed jars and had even torn out pages from obscure gardening magazines that advertised sources for such containers. He had ordered them. She had also drawn in a lattice work of trellises for sweet peas and green beans and morning glories — no espaliered fruit trees, however.

You have a problem with that?

Of course I do . . . nothing like nailing a perfectly good fruit tree to a wall. . . .

"Oh my God, Tristan, the arbor looks gorgeous!" Ceil exclaimed from across the way where she had walked with Adams. "It's like a waterfall of white roses."

Yes, thought Tristan. And the peonies — *like show girls — outrageous!*

Judith Stein came over and put a hand on his arm. "Anything I can do?" Tristan shook his head. Ceil and Judith began to speak in gentle murmuring tones as Tristan walked toward the peonies. He stopped at the *Astilbe grandis,* under the copper beech. *Why are you crying, Maggie?* They seemed a bit ahead of schedule; showing a little white, almost like a mist creeping in.

A calm began to steal over Tristan for the first time in months. Some guests were arriving along with the priest from Holy Redeemer. He should greet them but he had just caught a glimpse of blue and began to walk in that direction. It seemed impossible, but the tiny blossoms of the blue ridge phlox that he had suggested planting the first time they had night gardened were out. They never bloomed this early. He walked on toward the wildflower garden — *with wild anything, I guess, there is not always a relationship between beauty and rarity* . . .

Then he stopped. "No!" he whispered.

Yes!

The old damask rose quivered in the breeze, blood red, its petals still dewy as if it had just opened in the dawn. Tristan turned slowly around. The dogwood, which should have gone by days before, spread its blossoming branches just as it had on the first night they had made love. It beckoned now down the *roji* path. Somehow time had slipped its moorings, seasons had stayed or come early. All was wick. With each step, Tristan felt the glow of her presence. It filled the garden. He could smell the jasmine already from the second step garden, a stand of bell song daffodils, the cups the same color as her nipples, bloomed again. The three step gardens appeared as if in one single moment. A scarlet leaf drifted down and landed on his shirt. He remembered. Oh, how he remembered — once upon a time, another scarlet leaf against her porcelain skin. He plucked this one from his sleeve and there was a laugh that came on the breeze. "Oh, Flaherty!" he said, sighing.